Tonight He Met The Most Beautiful He'd Ever Seen

A woman who looked totally out of place in Gamble, Wyoming. A woman whose voice alone could stir something deep inside of him.

A woman who was already taken.

There was no denying he was attracted to her, but wanting her was taboo. So why was he thinking about her even now? And why in the hell was he so eager to see her again tomorrow?

Dear Reader,

When I introduced the Westmorelands with Delaney's story almost eight years ago, I never thought that it would go beyond the twelve stories that included Delaney and her eleven siblings and cousins. Then I introduced Uncle Corey and had to acquaint him with the triplets he never knew existed. Twelve books then became fifteen books.

And no, I'm not finished yet!

Meet the Westmorelands of Denver, Colorado, who are long-lost cousins to our Atlanta group. The men are just as hot and the women are just as stubborn. They are Westmorelands through and through, and I hope you have fun reading their stories and watching how they find true and everlasting love.

The oldest of the Denver clan is Dillon, a man who has tried marriage before, discovered it wasn't for him and has no intentions of trying it again. At least that was his intent before he met Pamela Novak. He finds staying a bachelor is no longer an option, but he's faced with numerous challenges before he can make her his. But this Denver Westmoreland won't let anything stand in his way—not even Pamela's fiancé.

Thank you for making the Westmorelands a very special family and I look forward to bringing you more books of searing desire and endless love and passion.

Happy reading!

Brenda Jackson

BRENDA JACKSON

WESTMORELAND'S WAY

Silhouette® Desire

Published by Silhouette Books

America's Publisher of Contemporary Romance

If you purchased this book without a cover you should be aware
that this book is stolen property. It was reported as "unsold and
destroyed" to the publisher, and neither the author nor the
publisher has received any payment for this "stripped book."

To my husband, the love of my life
and my best friend, Gerald Jackson, Sr.
To everyone who enjoys reading a Brenda Jackson novel,
this one is for you!

Ponder the path of thy feet, and let all thy ways be established.
—*Proverbs* 4:26

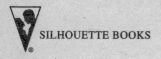

SILHOUETTE BOOKS

Recycling programs
for this product may
not exist in your area.

ISBN-13: 978-0-373-76975-9

WESTMORELAND'S WAY

Copyright © 2009 by Brenda Streater Jackson

All rights reserved. Except for use in any review, the reproduction
or utilization of this work in whole or in part in any form by any
electronic, mechanical or other means, now known or hereafter
invented, including xerography, photocopying and recording, or in
any information storage or retrieval system, is forbidden without
the written permission of the editorial office, Silhouette Books,
233 Broadway, New York, NY 10279 U.S.A.

This is a work of fiction. Names, characters, places and incidents are
either the product of the author's imagination or are used fictitiously, and
any resemblance to actual persons, living or dead, business establishments,
events or locales is entirely coincidental.

This edition published by arrangement with Harlequin Books S.A.

® and TM are trademarks of Harlequin Books S.A., used under license.
Trademarks indicated with ® are registered in the United States Patent
and Trademark Office, the Canadian Trade Marks Office and in other
countries.

Visit Silhouette Books at www.eHarlequin.com

Printed in U.S.A.

Books by Brenda Jackson

BRENDA JACKSON

is a die "heart" romantic who married her childhood sweetheart and still proudly wears the "going steady" ring he gave her when she was fifteen. Because she's always believed in the power of love, Brenda's stories all have happy endings. In her real-life love story, Brenda and her husband of thirty-six years live in Jacksonville, Florida, and have two sons.

A *New York Times* bestselling author of more than fifty romance titles, Brenda is a recent retiree who worked thirty-seven years in management at a major insurance company. She divides her time between family, writing and traveling with Gerald. You may write Brenda at P.O. Box 28267, Jacksonville, Florida 32226, by e-mail at WriterBJackson@aol.com or visit her Web site at www.brendajackson.net.

THE DENVER WESTMORELAND FAMILY TREE

Raphel and Gemma Westmoreland

Stern Westmoreland (Paula Bailey)

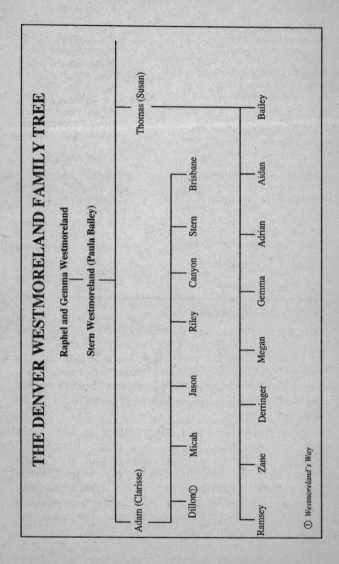

Adam (Clarisse)

Thomas (Susan)

Dillon①

Micah

Jason

Riley

Canyon

Stern

Brisbane

Ramsey

Zane

Derringer

Megan

Gemma

Adrian

Aidan

Bailey

① *Westmoreland's Way*

Prologue

"I know how much finding out everything there is about your grandfather means to you, and I wish you the best in that endeavor. If you ever need anything, you, your brothers and cousins should know that the Atlanta Westmorelands are here. Call on us at any time."

Dillon Westmoreland drained his wineglass before meeting the older man's eyes. He'd only met James Westmoreland eleven months ago. He had arrived in Denver, Colorado, with his sons and nephews, claiming to be his kin. They'd had the documentation to prove it.

"Thank you, sir," Dillon said. Their unexpected appearance at the Shady Tree Ranch had answered a lot of questions, but generated even more. After years of thinking they had no living relatives outside of Denver, it was nice to know there were others—others who hadn't hesitated to claim them as their own.

Dillon glanced around the wedding reception given for his cousin Reggie and Reggie's wife, Olivia. Dillon and the other Denver Westmorelands had officially met Reggie with a bunch of other Westmorelands from Atlanta at the family reunion a few months before. All it took was one look to know they were related. Their facial features, complexions and builds were practically the same. No surprise, given the fact their great-grand-fathers, Reginald and Raphel, had been identical twins.

Dillon now knew the story of how his great-grand-father, Raphel Westmoreland, had split from the family at the age of twenty-two. He'd left Atlanta, Georgia, with the wife of the town's preacher. It had been con-sidered a despicable act and Raphel had immediately become known as the black sheep in the Westmoreland family, never to be heard from again.

Many assumed he had died before his twenty-fifth birthday with a bounty on his head for wife-stealing. Few knew that Raphel had eventually made it to Denver, married and produced a son who had given him two grandsons, who in turn had blessed him with fifteen great-grands. Dillon was proud to say, at thirty-six, he was the oldest of Raphel's great-grandchildren. That left the Denver Westmoreland's legacy right smack on Dillon's shoulders.

It hadn't been easy, but he had done his best to lead his family. And he hadn't done too badly. All fifteen of them were successful in their own right, even the three that were still in college. But then you had to really try hard to overlook his youngest brother, Bane, whose occasional brush with the law kept Dillon down at police headquarters more than he would have liked.

"Are you still determined to find out the truth about whatever happened to your great-grandfather's other wives, or whether his previous relationships were even wives at all?" James Westmoreland asked him.

"Yes, sir. I'm taking time off from my company later this year, sometime in November, to travel to Wyoming," Dillon said.

Through James Westmoreland's genealogy research he had found Dillon's family. Now it was up to the Denver Westmorelands to find answers to the questions that still plagued them about their ancestry. That was one of the reasons why the trip to Wyoming was so important to him.

"Okay, Dillon, Uncle James has had your ear long enough."

Dillon couldn't help but chuckle when his cousin Dare Westmoreland walked up. If there had been a doubt in anyone's mind that the Atlanta and Denver Westmorelands were related, all they had to do was to compare him to Dare. Their features were so similar they could have been born brothers instead of cousins.

"I don't mind," he said truthfully. "I'm enjoying myself."

"Well, don't have too much fun," Dare responded with a huge grin. "As soon as Reggie and Olivia leave for their honeymoon, we're heading over to Chase's Place for a game of poker."

Dillon raised a brow. "The last time I played poker with you all, I almost lost the shirt off my back," he said, unable to suppress a grin.

Dare gave him a huge pat on that back. "All I can say to that, Dillon, is welcome to the family."

One

"Have you totally lost your mind, Pam? No matter what you say, we can't let you do it. You've given up so much for us already. We just can't."

Pamela Novak smiled as she glanced over her shoulder and saw the three militant faces frowning at her and quickly decided it would be best to give them her full attention. Drying her hands on a towel she turned away from the sink to face them.

She wondered what it would take to make her sisters see reason and understand that she had to do what she had to do. Not just for her own benefit but mainly for theirs. Fletcher was pushing for a Christmas wedding and here it was the first week in November already. So far they hadn't set a date, but he would bring it up every time she saw him. He'd let it be known that he didn't want a long engagement and, considering everything, a long engagement wouldn't be in her best interest, either.

She nibbled on her bottom lip, trying to come up with a quick yet effective strategy. If she could convince her sister Jillian of the importance of what she had to do, then Paige and Nadia would quickly come on board. But convincing Jillian was the big challenge. Jill didn't like Fletcher.

"And what makes you think it's something I'm being forced to do, rather than something I want to do?" Pamela finally decided to ask the three of them.

Of course, it was Jillian who stepped out to speak. Jill, as she was called by most people in Gamble, Wyoming, at seventeen was a senior in high school and was a spitfire. She was also smart as a whip. It was Pam's most fervent desire for Jill to leave Gamble next fall to attend the University of Wyoming in Laramie and pursue her dream of one day becoming a neurosurgeon.

And Paige, fifteen, and Nadia, thirteen, would soon be ready to pursue their aspirations. Pam wanted to make sure that funds were available for college when that time came. She also wanted to make sure that if her sisters wanted to return to Gamble, they would still have a home here. Pam felt certain that accepting Fletcher's marriage proposal made those things possible.

"You're sacrificing your happiness, Pam. We aren't stupid. What woman in her right mind would want to marry a jerk like Fletcher Mallard?" Jill boldly said.

Pam had to fight to keep a straight face when she said, "He is not a jerk. In fact, Fletcher is a nice man."

"When he's not being obnoxious and arrogant, which is most of the time. Already he thinks he can run things around here. We've been doing just fine without him," was Jill's bitter response.

Jill took a quick breather and then went on to say, "We don't care if we lose this house and it wouldn't bother us in the least if we don't get a college education. We refuse to let you marry the likes of *that* man to protect what you see as our bright futures. Speaking of futures, you should be back in California working on a real movie instead of spending your time teaching students at the acting school. You got a degree in drama, Pam. Being an actress has always been your dream. Your passion. You shouldn't have given it up for us."

Pam inhaled deeply. She had been through all of this before with her sisters. The problem was that they knew too much about the situation, something she wished hadn't happened. Unfortunately for her, they had been home that day when Lester Gadling, her father's attorney, had dropped by to deliver the bad news and they had overheard Lester's words.

"But I'm not in California. I'm perfectly satisfied being here in Gamble and running the acting school, giving others the same opportunity that was given to me," she countered.

She paused for a second and then said, "Listen, ladies, I've made these decisions because I love you."

"And we love you, too, Pammie," Nadia replied. "But

we can't let you give up the chance to one day meet a really nice guy and—"

"Fletcher is a nice guy," she interjected. However, all she received for her effort were three pairs of rolling eyes.

"No, he's not," Paige spoke up to say. "I was in the bank one day when he went off on one of the tellers for making him wait in line for so long. He thinks he's all that, just because he owns a chain of grocery stores."

"Okay, you saw his bad side just that one time," Pam said. "Deep down he's a kind person. He's willing to help us out, isn't he?"

"Yes, but look what he'll be getting. Our home and the most beautiful single woman in Gamble," Jill pointed out.

"A single woman who isn't getting any younger and who will be turning thirty in a few months. Don't you think it's time I get married?"

"Yes, but not to him," Jill implored. "Anyone but him."

Pam glanced at the kitchen clock that hung on the wall. Fletcher was coming to dinner and would be arriving any minute, and she needed to make sure her sisters put this behind them. They had to accept that she was now an engaged woman and move on.

She of all people knew that Fletcher had his flaws and could be arrogant at times, but she could deal with that. What she refused to deal with was letting her sisters lose the only home they knew and a chance to fulfill their dreams by attending the colleges they desired.

She couldn't help but wonder what her father had been thinking to put a second mortgage on their home—

a mortgage for which the full balance was due within a year of his death. There was no way she could come up with a million dollars. Fletcher, in the role of a friend, had made her an offer that she couldn't refuse. It would not be a love match, he was fully aware of that. She would, however, as agreed, perform her wifely duties. He wanted kids one day and so did she. And Pam was determined to make the most of their marriage and be a good wife to him.

"I want the three of you to make me a promise," she finally said to her sisters.

"What kind of promise?" Jill asked, lifting a suspicious brow.

"I want you to promise me that you will do everything I ask regarding my engagement to Fletcher. That, you will make me, as your oldest sister, happy by supporting my marriage to him."

"But will you be truly happy, Pammie?" Paige asked with an expression that said she really had to know.

No, she wouldn't *truly* be happy, but her sisters didn't have to know that, Pam thought. They must never know the extent of her sacrifice for them. With that resolve in mind, Pam lifted her chin, looked all three of them in the eyes and told a lie that she knew was going to be well worth it in the end.

"Yes," she said, plastering a fake smile on her lips. "I will truly be happy. I want to marry Fletcher. Now, make me that promise."

Jill, Paige and Nadia hesitated only for a moment and then said simultaneously, "We promise."

"Good."

When Pam turned back to the sink, the three girls looked at each other and smiled. Their fingers had been crossed behind their backs when they'd made their promise.

It was probably inconsiderate of him to show up without calling first, Dillon thought, as he turned into the long driveway that was marked as the Novak Homestead.

He had arrived in Gamble, Wyoming, earlier that day, with his mission on his mind. What had happened to his great-grandfather's other four wives, the ones he had before he married Dillon's great-grandmother, Gemma? According to the genealogy research James Westmoreland had done, Gamble was the first place Raphel had settled in after leaving Atlanta, and a man by the name of Jay Novak had been his business partner in a dairy business.

Dillon would have called, but he couldn't get a signal on his cell phone. Roy Davis, the man who owned the only hotel in Gamble, had explained that was because Gamble was in such a rural area, getting a good signal was almost impossible. Dillon had shaken his head. It was absurd that in this day and age there was a town in which you couldn't get a decent cell signal when you needed it.

He had finally gotten a signal earlier to contact his secretary to check on things back at the office. Not surprisingly, everything was under control, since he had hired the right people to make sure his billion-dollar real estate firm continued to be a success whether or not he was there.

Dillon parked his car behind another car in the yard and glanced up at a huge Victorian house with a shingle roof. It was very similar in design to his home in Denver and he wondered if that was a coincidence.

According to what he'd heard, four sisters occupied the house and the oldest was named Pamela Novak. He understood Ms. Novak had had an up-and-coming acting career in California but had moved back to Gamble upon her father's death. She was now operating the drama school a former teacher had recently willed to her.

When Dillon got out of the rental car he took time to stretch his legs. Like most Westmorelands he was tall, and because of his height he'd always enjoyed playing basketball. He'd been set to begin a career in the NBA when he'd gotten word of the plane crash that had claimed the lives of his parents and his aunt and uncle, leaving fourteen younger Westmorelands in his care.

It hadn't been easy and Tammi, his girlfriend from college, had claimed she would stick by his side no matter what. Less than six months into their marriage she had run back home hollering and screaming that she couldn't handle living on a ranch with a bunch of heathens.

That was after she had failed to convince him to put his youngest brother, Bane, who'd been eight at the time, his cousins—Adrian and Aiden—the twins who'd been ten, and Bailey, who'd been seven, into foster care because they were always getting into some kind of mischief.

He had understood that most of their antics had been

for the attention they'd needed after losing their parents. However, Tammi had failed to see it that way and wanted out of the marriage. One good thing that had come out of his divorce was that he'd realized it was meant for him to be single and, as long as he was the head of the family, he would stay that way.

Another good thing about his divorce was that the younger Westmorelands—all of them with the exception of Bane—had felt guilty about Tammi leaving and had improved their behavior. Now the twins and Bailey were in college. Bane…was still Bane.

"You lost, mister?"

Dillon quickly turned around to look into two pairs of dark brown eyes standing a few yards away. Twins? No, but they could pass for such. Now he could see that one of the teenage girls was a head taller than the other.

"Well, are you?"

He smiled. Evidently he hadn't spoken quick enough to suit them. "No, I'm not lost if this is the Novaks' place."

The taller of the two said, "I'm a Novak. We both are."

Dillon chuckled. "Then I guess I'm at the right place."

"Who did you want to see?"

"I want to see Pamela Novak."

The shorter of the two nodded. "That's our sister. She's in the house talking to *him*."

Dillon raised a brow. He had no idea who *him* was, and from the distasteful way it had been said, he really wasn't sure he wanted to find out. "If she's busy I can come back later," he said, moving back toward the car.

"Yeah, because he might get mad if he thought you'd come calling just to see Pammie," the taller one said.

A look of mischief shone in their eyes as the two girls looked at each other and smiled. And then, screaming to the top of their voices, they called, "Pammie, a man is here to see you!"

Dillon leaned against his car with arms across his chest, knowing he had been set up, and the two teens were having a little fun at his expense. He wasn't so sure how he liked it until the door to the house swung open. At that moment he literally forgot to breathe. A strikingly beautiful woman walked out. It didn't matter that she was frowning. The only thing that mattered was that she was definitely the living, breathing specimen of the most gorgeous woman he'd ever seen.

She couldn't have been any taller than five-eight, and was slim with just the right curves in the jeans she was wearing. She had shoulder-length black hair flowing around her shoulders and a medium brown complexion that complimented the rest of her features. Her eye color was the same dark brown as the two scamps, and she had a pixie nose that was perfect for her face. She was definitely a stunner. A raven-haired beauty that made him nearly breathless.

"Hey, you're trespassing. May I help you?"

He looked beyond her to a big hulk of a man standing directly behind her in the doorway who'd asked the question in a high-pitched and agitated tone. And he was glaring at Dillon as if his very presence annoyed the hell out of him.

Dillon quickly figured that this must be the "him" the girls had been referring to, and was about to open his mouth to speak when the taller of the two girls spoke up. "No, you can't help him because he didn't come to see you, Fletcher. He came to see Pammie."

A dark scowl covered the man's face at the same time a smile touched the teen's lips. It wasn't hard to see she was deliberately trying to get a rise out of the man.

"Paige and Nadia, shouldn't you be upstairs doing your homework?" the gorgeous woman asked the two before turning her curious gaze on Dillon. Unlike her male friend, she smiled brightly and had a cheerful look on her face.

"Pamela Novak?" he heard himself ask, trying to force air into his lungs. He'd seen beautiful women before, but there was something about her that was doing something to everything male within him.

"Yes," she said, still smiling while stepping down the steps toward him. He pushed away from the car and began moving toward her, as well.

"Wait a minute, Pamela," the hulk of a man called out. "You don't know this man. You shouldn't be so quick to be nice to people."

"Maybe you should follow her lead, Fletcher."

A new voice Dillon hadn't heard before had spoken up, entering the fray. He glanced behind the hulk to see a young woman, probably around seventeen or eighteen, stepping out the door. Another sister, he quickly surmised, due to the similarities in their features.

Pamela Novak continued walking and when she

came to a stop in front of Dillon, she offered her hand. "Yes, I'm Pamela Novak, and you are…?"

He accepted her hand and immediately felt a warmth that began to flow all through his body. Then a fluttering he felt in the pit of his stomach began to slide downward. Even the engagement ring he'd noticed her wearing couldn't stop the sensations engulfing him.

He watched her mouth move, fascinated with her lips and thinking they had a nice shape. He felt his stomach tighten when he raised his gaze from her lips to her eyes. "I'm Dillon Westmoreland."

He watched her brow lift ever so slightly, although she kept her smile in place. He could tell she was searching her memory for when, how and where she recalled the last name. He decided to help her. "I understand that my great-grandfather, Raphel Westmoreland, was once a business partner of your great-grandfather, Jay Winston Novak."

The smile on her lips transformed into a full chuckle. "Oh, yes, Raphel Westmoreland. The wife stealer."

He couldn't stop his lips from twitching in a smile. "Yes, so I've heard. In fact, that's the reason I'm here. I—"

"What does he want, Pamela?"

Dillon could tell by the stiffening of Pamela Novak's shoulders that she wished the hulk would keep quiet for once. "Is he your fiancé?" he couldn't help asking.

She met his gaze and studied it for a moment before saying, "Yes."

She then inclined her head to call back over her shoulder, "This is Dillon Westmoreland. Our great-grandfathers were once business partners so I consider him a friend of the family."

She quickly turned back to Dillon, presented him with another smile and whispered, "You know I say that loosely, don't you, considering your great-grandfather's reputation."

Now it was Dillon's time to chuckle. "The reason I'm here is to find out all I can about that reputation since I only recently discovered he had one and—"

"What does he want, Pamela?"

Before she could respond the shortest of the teen imps said, "We already told you. He wants Pammie."

The hulk's frown deepened and Dillon knew the young girl hadn't meant it the way it sounded, but basically she had spoken the truth. He *was* attracted to Pamela Novak. Encroaching into another man's territory had been Raphel Westmoreland's style, but was not his. However, at that moment Dillon didn't feel any guilt about the thoughts going through his mind, especially since it was apparent the woman was engaged to an ass. But that was her business, not his.

The man came down the steps and moved toward them and Dillon quickly sized him up. He wore a suit and an expensive pair of black leather shoes. His shirt and tie didn't look cheap, either, which meant he was probably a successful businessman of some sort.

When he stopped in front of him, Dillon offered the man his hand. "I'm Dillon Westmoreland, and like Ms.

Novak said, I'm a family friend. The reason I'm here," he decided to add, "is because I'm doing research on my family's history."

The man shook his hand. "And I'm Fletcher Mallard, Pamela's fiancé," he said, as if he needed to stake a claim by speaking his position out loud.

Dillon took it in stride and thought that you could tell a lot about a man from his handshake, and this man had all the telltale signs. He was using the squeezing handshake, often used to exert strength and power. A confident man didn't need such a tactic. This man was insecure.

Mallard looked at Dillon skeptically. "And just what is it you want to know?"

The smile dropped from Pamela Novak's lips and she actually glared at her fiancé. "There's no reason for you to ask all these questions, Fletcher. Mr. Westmoreland is a family friend and that's all that matters right now."

As if her words settled it, she turned to Dillon with her smile back in place. "Mr. Westmoreland, please join us for dinner, then you can tell me how we can help in your quest to learn more of your family's history."

It would have been so easy and less complicated to decline her offer, but there was something about Fletcher Mallard that outright irritated Dillon and pushed him to accept her invitation.

"Thank you, Ms. Novak, and I'd love to stay for dinner."

Two

Pam knew she had made a mistake inviting Dillon Westmoreland to dinner the moment he was seated at the table. She wished she could say Fletcher was in rare form, but she'd seen him behave this way before, when another man had shown interest in her.

But what was strange was that Dillon hadn't actually shown any interest in her, so she couldn't understand why Fletcher was being so territorial. Unless...he had picked up on her interest in Dillon.

She pushed such utter nonsense from her mind. She was *not* interested in Dillon. She was merely curious. What woman wouldn't be interested in a man like Dillon Westmoreland. He was at least six foot four with coffee-colored features. He had an angular face that boasted a firm jaw, a pair of cute dimples, full lips and the darkest eyes she'd ever seen on a man. She was engaged to be married, but not blind. And when he had sat down at the table to join them for dinner, his presence was powerfully masculine in a distracting way. She glanced around the table and couldn't help noticing her sisters' fascination with him, as well.

"So just where are you from, Westmoreland?"

Her spine stiffened with Fletcher's question. She hadn't invited Dillon to dinner to be interrogated, but she knew Fletcher wouldn't be satisfied until he got some answers. She also knew once he got them he still wouldn't be contented.

"I'm from Denver," Dillon answered.

Fletcher was about to ask another question when Dillon beat him to the punch. "And where are you from, Mallard?"

The question had clearly caught Fletcher off guard. He had a way of trying to intimidate people, but she had a feeling that Dillon Westmoreland was a man who couldn't be intimidated.

"I'm from Laramie," Fletcher said gruffly. "I moved to town about five years ago to open a grocery store here. That was my first. Since then I've opened over twenty more in other cities in Wyoming and Montana. It's my goal to have a Mallard Super Store in every state in the union over the next five years."

Pam couldn't help but inwardly smile. If Fletcher thought that announcement would get a reaction from

Dillon, then he was sadly mistaken. Dillon didn't show any sign that he was the least impressed.

"Where are you staying while you're in town?" Fletcher asked, helping himself to the mashed potatoes.

"At the River's Edge Hotel."

"Nice place if you can do without cable television," Jill said, smiling.

Pam watched how easily Dillon returned Jill's smile. "I can do without it. I don't watch much television."

"And what is it that you do?" Fletcher asked in a voice that Pam felt was as cold as the iced tea she was drinking.

Dillon, she saw, gave Fletcher a smile that didn't quite reach his eyes when he said, "I'm into real estate."

"Oh, you sell homes," Fletcher said as if the occupation was beneath him.

"Not quite," Dillon said pleasantly. "I own a real estate firm. You might have heard of it, Blue Ridge Land Management."

Pam saw the surprise that lit Fletcher's eyes before he said, "Yes, I've heard of it."

She had to force back a chuckle because she was sure that he had heard of it. Who hadn't? The Blue Ridge Land Management Company was a billion-dollar corporation, well known in the Mountain States, that had a higher place on the Fortune 500 list than Mallard Super Stores.

Seeing that Fletcher was momentarily speechless, she stepped in to say, "Mr. Westmoreland, you said that—"

"I'm Dillon."

He had raised his gaze to meet hers and she saw a friendly smile lurking in the dark depths of his eyes. Her heart rate began accelerating in her chest. "Yes, of course," she said quickly. "And I'm Pam."

After taking a sip of her tea, she continued. "Dillon, you said that you were here to research your family's history?"

"Yes," he said, his gaze still on her. "For years I was told by my parents and grandparents that my brothers, cousins and I didn't have any living relatives, and that my great-grandfather, Raphel Westmoreland, had been an only child. So you could imagine my surprise when one day, out of the clear blue sky, a man, his two sons and three nephews showed up at my ranch to proclaim they were my kin."

Intrigued by the story, Pam placed her fork next to her plate and gave him her full attention. "How did they find you?"

"Through a genealogy search. The older man, James Westmoreland, knew that his grandfather, Reginald Westmoreland, had an identical-twin brother. It was discovered that that twin brother was my great-grandfather, Raphel, who had left home at twenty-two and had never been heard from again. In fact, the family assumed he'd died. They had no idea that he had eventually settled in Denver, married and had a son, who gave him two grandsons and then a slew of great-grands—fifteen, in fact. I am the oldest of the fifteen great-grands."

"Wow, that must have been a shocker for you to

discover you had other relatives when you assumed there weren't any," Jill, who was practically hanging on to Dillon's every word, said. "What does your wife think about all of this?"

Pam watched Dillon smile and knew he hadn't been fooled by the way the question had been asked. Jill wanted to know if he was a married man. Pam hated to admit that she was just as curious. He wasn't wearing a ring, but that didn't necessarily mean a thing.

"She didn't have anything to say because I'm not married," Dillon replied smoothly. "At least not anymore. I've been divorced for close to ten years."

Pam glanced over at Jill and prayed her sister had the decency not to inquire as to what had happened to end his marriage.

Fletcher, disliking the fact he wasn't the center of attention, spoke up in an authoritative negative voice. "Sounds pretty crazy to me. Why would you care about a bunch of people who show up at your place claiming they were your relatives, or better yet, why would you want to find out your family history? You should live in the present and not in the past."

Pam could tell Dillon was fighting hard to hold his temper in check, and his tone was remarkably restrained when he finally responded. "Do you have a family, Fletcher?"

Again, by Fletcher's expression it was obvious he didn't appreciate being the one receiving the questions. "No, I was an only child. My parents are deceased, but they didn't have any siblings, either. I'm the only

Mallard around for now." He glanced over at Pam and smiled. "Of course, that will change once Pamela and I marry."

Dillon nodded slowly. "But until that changes, I wouldn't expect you to understand the significance of what a family means. I already do. Westmorelands are big into family and, after meeting my other relatives, my only regret is not having known them sooner."

He glanced over at her and, for a second, she held his steady gaze. And she felt it. There was a connection between them that they were trying to ignore. She looked down at her plate as she continued eating.

Nadia asked him a question about his siblings and just as comfortably and easily as a man who was confident with himself and who he was, he began telling her everything she wanted to know. Without even trying, Dillon was captivating everyone at the dinner table… with the exception of Fletcher.

"How long do you plan to stay in town?" Fletcher rudely cut into the conversation between Dillon and the sisters.

Dillon glanced over at Fletcher. "Until I get all the questions I have about Raphel Westmoreland answered."

"That may take a while," Fletcher said.

Dillon smiled, but Pam knew it was just for Fletcher's benefit and it wasn't sincere. "I got time."

She saw Fletcher open his mouth to make another statement and she cut him off. "Dillon, I should be able to help you with that. My great-grandfather's old business records, as well as his personal journal, are in the attic. If you want to drop by tomorrow and go up there and look around, you're welcome to do so."

"Thanks," he said, smiling. "I'll be happy to take you up on your offer."

"I don't want you meeting with that man alone, Pamela. Inviting him here tomorrow while your sisters are away at school wasn't a good idea. And tomorrow I'll be out of town visiting my stores in Laramie."

Pam glanced over at Fletcher as she walked him to the door. He was upset and she knew it. In fact, there was no doubt in her mind that everyone at the dinner table had known it since he wasn't a person who hid his emotions well.

"So," he continued, "I'll get word to him tomorrow that you've withdrawn the invitation."

Fletcher's words stopped her dead in her tracks just a few feet from her living room door. She stared at him, certain she had missed something, like a vital piece of their conversation, somewhere along the way. "Excuse me?"

"I said that since you agree that you shouldn't be alone with Westmoreland, I'll get word to him that you've withdrawn your invitation for tomorrow."

She frowned. "I don't agree to any such nonsense. The invitation I gave to Dillon Westmoreland still stands, Fletcher. You're acting controlling and territorial and there's no reason for it."

She saw the muscle that ticked in his jaw, indicating he was angry. "You're an attractive woman, Pamela. Westmoreland isn't blind. He noticed," he said.

"And what is that supposed to mean? I agreed to marry you but that doesn't mean you own me. If you're having seconds thoughts about this engagement, then—"

"Of course I'm not having second thoughts. I'm just trying to look out for you, that's all. You're too trusting with people."

His gaze then flicked over her before returning to her face. "And I think that you're the one having second thoughts," he said.

She lifted her chin. "Of course I'm having second thoughts. I agreed to marry you as a way to save my ranch. I appreciate you coming to my rescue but you deserve better than that. And that's why I plan to pay Lester Gadling another visit this week. I want him to go back over those papers. It's hard to believe Dad did not make arrangements for the balance on that mortgage to be paid off if anything happened to him."

Fletcher waited for a moment, then said, "If you feel that strongly about it then I agree that you should go back to Gadling, since he was your father's attorney, and ask him about it. But don't worry about what I deserve. I'll have you as my wife and that will make me a happy man."

Pamela didn't say anything. She and Fletcher weren't entering into their marriage under false assumptions. He knew she was not in love with him.

She took a moment to reflect on a few things. She had left home upon graduating from high school with a full scholarship to attend the University of Southern California Drama School. It was during her sophomore year that Alma, her stepmother, had died. Her father had married Alma when Pam was ten, and Alma had been wonderful in filling the void after losing her mother.

She had thought about dropping out of college and returning home, but her father wouldn't hear of it. He was adamant about her staying in school and insisted that he would be able to care for her sisters, although Nadia had been only three at the time, the same age she'd been when she'd lost her own mother.

"Pamela?"

Pam blinked upon realizing Fletcher had called her name. "I'm sorry, Fletcher. I was just thinking about happier times, when Dad and Alma were both alive."

"And you will have even happier times once we're married, Pamela," he said, reaching out and taking her hand in his. "I know you don't love me now, but I'm convinced you will grow to love me. Just think of all the things I can give you."

She lifted her chin. "I'm not asking for you to give me all those things, Fletcher. The only things I've asked for, and that you've promised, are to make sure my sisters retain ownership of our home and to put my sisters through college."

"I promise all of that. And I'll promise to give you more if you would just let me," he said in a low, frustrated tone.

She didn't say anything for a long moment and knew her silence was probably grating on his nerves, but she couldn't help it. "I don't want anything more, Fletcher, so please let's just leave it at that."

Pam had met Fletcher four years ago on one of her trips back to Gamble to visit her family. After that, whenever she came to town, he would make it a point to ask her if she would go out with him.

After her father died and she'd moved back home, he had come calling on a regular basis, although she had explained to him that friendship was all there could ever be between them. At the time, he had seemed satisfied with that.

Then Lester Gadling had come visiting and dropped the bombshell that had changed her life forever. Fletcher had stopped by that evening and she had found herself telling him what had happened. He had listened attentively before presenting what he saw as an easy solution. She could marry him and her financial problems would be over.

At first, she'd thought he'd fallen off the deep end, certain he had taken leave of his senses. But the more she'd thought about it, the more his suggestion had taken shape in her mind. All she had to do was marry him and he would see to it that her ranch was saved and would establish a trust fund for her sisters, so when the time came for their college, everything would be set.

She didn't accept his offer at first, determined to handle things without Fletcher's help. She had gone to bank after bank trying to secure a loan but time and time again had been turned down. She had only accepted Fletcher's proposal when she'd seen she had no other choice.

Glancing down at her watch, she said, "It's getting late."

"All right. Don't forget to be careful around Westmoreland. There is something about him that I don't trust."

"Like I said, Fletcher, I'll be fine."

He nodded before leaning in closer to brush a kiss across her lips. As always she waited for blood to rush fast and furious through her veins, fire to suffuse her insides, but as usual, nothing happened. No stirring sensations. Not a single spark.

For months she had ignored the fact that she was not physically attracted to the man she was going to marry. It hadn't bothered her until tonight when she discovered she was *very* physically attracted to another man. And that man's name was Dillon Westmoreland.

Dillon eased his body into a huge bathtub filled with warm water. Whatever amenities the little hotel lacked, he would have to say a soak in this tub definitely made up for them. There weren't too many bathtubs around that could accommodate his height comfortably.

He closed his eyes and stretched out, thinking he'd never been able to relax in a tub before. It had been a while since he'd been able to sit in a tub and not worry about being disturbed by some family member needing his help or advice.

Family.

Damn, but he missed them already. He wasn't worried about the family he'd left in Denver since he'd left Ramsey in charge. He and Ramsey were only separated in age by seven months and were more like brothers than they were cousins. If truth be told, Ramsey was his best friend. Always had been and always would be.

He couldn't wait until he began digging into information about Raphel. He could have hired an agency to do it for him, but this was something he wanted to do himself. Something he felt he owed his family. If there was something in his great-grandfather's past, then he felt he should be the one to uncover it. Good or bad.

Dillon shifted his body. He kept his eyes closed while thinking that tonight he'd met the most beautiful woman he'd ever seen in his life. A woman who looked totally out of place in Gamble, Wyoming. A woman whose voice alone could stir something deep inside of him.

A woman who was already taken.

There was no denying he was attracted to her, but wanting her was taboo. So why was he thinking about her even now? And why in the hell was he so eager to see her again tomorrow?

He inhaled deeply, wondering how Fletcher Mallard could get so lucky. It was easy to see the man was a jerk, a pompous pain in the ass. But Fletcher was no concern of his, and neither was the man's engagement to Pamela Novak. Dillon was in Gamble for one thing and for one thing only. He was there to find out everything he could about Raphel, and not to encroach on another man's property.

He would do well to remember that.

Three

Glancing out the window Pam saw Dillon's car the moment it pulled up in front of the house. She took a sip of her coffee while watching him, grateful that the window was designed in a way that gave her a view of anyone arriving. From what she'd been told, her great-grandfather had deliberately built the house that way to have an advantage over anyone who came calling without their knowledge.

Today she was making full use of that advantage.

After he brought the car to a stop, she watched as he opened the car and got out. He stood for a moment to study her home, which gave her an opportunity to study him.

He was tall—she'd noticed that last night. But last night she hadn't had time to fully check him out. She couldn't help but appreciate what she saw now. Nice shoulders. Firm abdomen. Muscled chest. Taut thighs. He was wearing jeans and a blue western shirt that revealed strong arms, and a black Stetson was on his head.

She sighed deeply, thinking that inviting him to come back today might not have been a good idea after all, just as Fletcher had claimed. She glanced down at her hand holding the coffee cup and couldn't miss the diamond ring on her finger, the one Fletcher had put there a week ago.

Okay, so she was an engaged woman, one who would be marrying a nice guy in a few months. But being engaged, or married for that matter, didn't mean she couldn't appreciate a fine specimen of a man when she saw one. Besides, her best friend from college, Iris Michaels, would give her hell if she didn't check him out and then call to give her all the hot-tamale details.

She blinked as she nearly burnt her tongue on a sip of coffee when Dillon looked straight at her through what she'd always considered her secret window. How had he known about the side view? To anyone else it would appear to be a flat wall in the shadow of a huge oak tree.

There was only one way to find out. She pushed her chair away from the table and stood. As she made her way out of the kitchen toward the living room, she decided maybe it would be better for him not to know she'd been sitting here watching him since he'd arrived.

She slowly opened the door and was afforded an opportunity to watch him unseen some more when his attention was diverted by a flock of geese in the sky. While he studied the geese, she again studied him, taking in the angle of his face while his head was tilted slightly backward. He was standing with his legs braced apart and with his hands in his pockets. There was something about that stance, that particular pose—especially on him—that made her just want to stand there and stare.

While living in Los Angeles for five years she'd been surrounded by jaw-droppingly, stomach-stirringly handsome men, many from some of the world's most elite modeling agencies. But none could hold a light to the man presently standing in her yard. His features were distinct—sharp facial bones, firm jaw and full lips. His hair beneath his Stetson was close cut and trimmed neatly around his head.

A moment passed. Possibly two. When suddenly he turned his head and looked over in her direction.

She had been caught.

And she was immediately enveloped in his intense gaze. She was unable to do anything but return his stare while wondering why she was doing so. Why were her senses, her entire being, homed in on everything about him? This wasn't good, she thought.

At least that was what her mind was telling her, but her common sense hadn't gotten there yet. It was being held captive within the scope of the darkest pair of eyes she'd ever seen.

Somewhere in the not-too-faraway distance she

heard the sound of a car backfiring and the sound ripped right into the moment. It was only then that she was able to slide her gaze away from his to look over across the wide expanse of yard.

After taking a deep breath she returned her gaze to his, wrestled with those same senses she had lost control of earlier, placed a smile on her face and said, "Good morning, Dillon."

She wasn't just off the boat, and knew that during the brief moment when their gazes had held, something had happened. Just as it had last night. She wasn't sure of what, but she knew that it had. She also knew she would pretend that it hadn't. "It's a beautiful day, isn't it?" she added.

"Yes, it is," he said, turning to walk over toward her. Holy cow! she thought, swallowing deeply. The man's strides were sure, confident and deliberately masculine. He had one hell of a sexy walk, and what was so disturbing about it was that it seemed as natural as the sun rising in the morning.

He came to a stop in front of her and met her gaze fleetingly before glancing up at the sun. His gaze then returned to her. "It might rain later, though."

She nodded. "Yes, it might." She knew they were trying to get back in sync and to lessen the intensity of what had passed between them.

"I hope I'm not too early," he said in a deep, husky voice, breaking into her thoughts.

"No, you're fine. I was just having my morning coffee. Would you like to join me?"

With an ultrasexy shrug of his massive shoulders, he smiled as he removed his hat. "Umm, I don't know. I feel I'm taking a lot of your time already."

"No problem. Besides, you want to know about Raphel, right?"

"Yes. Is there something you can tell me other than he was your great-grandfather's partner and that he ran off with your great-grandmother, Portia Novak?"

Pam chuckled as she led him through the house and headed toward the kitchen. "Portia wasn't my great-grandmother," she corrected. "A few years after she'd run off, he met my great-grandmother and they married."

When he sat down at the table, she said, "I'm sure you've heard some stories about Raphel and Portia." She proceeded to pour him a cup of coffee.

"No, in actuality, I hadn't. I'd always assumed my great-grandmother Gemma was my great-grandfather's only wife. It was only after my Atlanta Westmoreland relatives showed up and explained how we were related that I found out about Portia Novak and the others."

Pam lifted a brow. "There were others?"

He nodded. "Yes, Gemma was his fifth wife."

Dillon was more than curious about what had happened to a preacher's wife, a woman by the name of Lila Elms. Although she was already legally married to the preacher, had she and Raphel pretended to be married for a spell before he dumped her for Portia, the wife of Jay Novak?

And then what happened to Clarice, wife number three? And Isabelle, wife four? All four women's names were rumored to be connected to Raphel in some say. If what they'd discovered so far was true, Raphel had taken up with the four women before his thirty-second birthday, and all had been married to another man or engaged to marry someone else. It seemed Raphel's reputation as a wife stealer was legendary.

Dillon took a sip of coffee, deciding for the moment not to inform her that the others, like Portia, were women who belonged to other men, legally or otherwise. But he would throw out the name of one she might have heard about already. "My goal is to find out what happened to Lila Elms."

"The preacher's wife?"

So, she had heard about Lila. "Yes." He took another sip and then asked, "How do you know so much about this stuff?"

She chuckled as she sat down at the table with him after refilling her own cup of coffee. "My grandmother. As a little girl we would spend hours and hours on the porch outside shelling peas, and she would fill my ears about all the family history. But the one subject she didn't shed a lot of light on was Portia. For some reason, any conversation about her was taboo. Jay wanted it that way and my great-grandmother respected his wishes."

Dillon nodded, trying to concentrate on what she was saying and not on how smoothly her lips would part each time she took a sip of her coffee. How the bottom lip would hang open a little and how the top one would fit perfectly around the rim of the cup.

He felt his gut tightening and took a sip of his coffee.

When he had been standing out in her yard and he'd turned and seen her staring at him, he had tried not to speculate just what was going on in her mind. He didn't want to even consider the possibility that it had been close to what had been going on in his.

Her gaze had touched him deeply, in a way he doubted she even realized. Something about Pamela Novak was calling out to him in the most elemental way, and that wasn't good. Since his divorce, he had dated on occasion. But if the truth be told, he'd made it a point to date only women who, like him, weren't interested in anything long term. All of those women had been unattached.

"Are you ready to go up to the attic?"

Her question reined his thoughts back and he glanced over at her and immediately wished he hadn't. Every muscle in his body immediately seemed to weaken yet at the same time fill him with an intensity that made him draw in a long breath. It was time to acknowledge it for what it was. Sexual chemistry.

He had heard about it but had never actually experienced it for himself. He'd been attracted to women before, but it never went further than an attraction. What he was beginning to feel was an element of something greater than a mere attraction. There were these primitive vibes he was not only emitting but was also receiving. That meant Pamela Novak was in tune to what was going on between them, although she might choose to pretend otherwise. Of course, he understood her reluctance to acknowledge such a thing. After all, she was an engaged woman. And she didn't come across as one who would deliberately be unfaithful to her fiancé.

But still…

"Yes, I'm ready," he finally said. "But first I want to clear the air about something." He watched her lips quiver nervously before she set her cup down and met his gaze. He tensed, trying to ignore the sensations rolling through him every time their eyes met.

"Clear the air about what?"

He'd been too busy watching her lips to pay any attention to the words flowing out of them. He fought back the urge to lift the tip of his finger and run it across those lips.

He cleared his throat. "About last night. My showing up here without calling first. I think I may have rattled your fiancé a little, and I regret doing that. It was not my intent to cause any problems between the two of you."

He watched as her shoulders gave a feminine shrug. "You didn't cause any problems. Don't worry about it."

She then stood. "I think we should go up to the attic and see what's there. There's a trunk that contains a lot of my great-grandfather's business records."

Dillon nodded. She had responded to his question and in the same breath, had effectively switched topics, which let him know the subject of her relationship with Fletcher Mallard was not up for discussion.

He pushed his chair back and then got on his feet. "I'm ready, just lead the way."

She did and he couldn't help but appreciate the backside that strolled in front of him as he followed.

* * *

With his long legs, it didn't take Dillon long to catch up with her, Pamela thought. Not that she was trying to leave him behind. But for a few moments she'd needed to get her bearings. The man had a way of making her not think straight.

He was silent as she led him up the stairs and she couldn't help looking sideways to gaze at his profile. What was it about him that affected her in a way Fletcher didn't? Her heart rate accelerated when she noticed he even climbed the stairs with an ingrained sexiness that made her senses reel.

When they reached the top landing he moved slightly ahead of her, as if he knew where he was going. "If I didn't know better I'd swear you've been here before," she said as they continued to walk toward the end of the hall that led to the attic stairs.

He glanced down at her and smiled. "This might sound crazy but this house is very similar to mine back in Denver. Was it built by your great-grandfather?"

"Yes."

"Then that might explain things, since the house I live in was built by Raphel. I'm thinking he liked the design, and when he decided to build his home he did so from his memory of this one."

"That would explain how you knew about our secret window." She regretted the words the moment they left her lips. She had just admitted to spying on him out the window when he'd arrived.

"Yes, that's how I know about it. I have one of my own just like it and in the same place."

"I see." But, in a way, she didn't see, which made her as eager to find out about Raphel as Dillon was.

She then walked on and he joined her. When they reached the door that led to the attic she opened it. Judging from the expression on his face, it was as if he'd seen the view before, and that made her determined to know why his home was a replica of hers.

Unlike the other stairs in her home, the attic steps were narrow and Dillon moved aside for her to go up ahead of him. She could feel the heat of his gaze on her back. She was tempted to glance over her shoulder but knew that wouldn't be the appropriate thing to do. So she did the next best thing and engaged him in conversation.

She broke into the silence by saying, "At dinner you mentioned that you were the oldest of Raphel's fifteen great-grands." She glanced briefly over her shoulder.

"Yes, and for a number of years I was the legal guardian for ten of them."

Pamela swung around so quickly, had she been standing on a stair she probably would have lost her balance. "Guardian to ten of them?"

At his nod, she blinked in amazement. "How did that come about?" She stepped aside when he reached her, noting there still wasn't a lot of room between them, but she was so eager to hear his answer she didn't make a move to step back any further.

"My parents and my aunt and uncle decided to go away for the weekend together, to visit one of my mother's friends in Louisiana. On their way back to Denver, their plane developed engine trouble and went down, killing everyone on board."

"Oh, how awful."

"Yes, it was. My parents had seven kids and my aunt and uncle had eight. I was the oldest at twenty-one. My brother Micah was nineteen and Jason was eighteen. My other brothers, Riley, Stern, Canyon and Brisbane, were all under sixteen."

He braced a hip against the stair railing and continued. "My cousin Ramsey was twenty, and his brother Zane was nineteen and Derringer was eighteen. The remaining cousins, Megan, Gemma, the twins Adrian and Aiden, and the youngest, Bailey, were also all under sixteen."

She also leaned against the rail to face him, still full of questions. "And family services didn't have a problem with you being responsible for so many little ones?"

"No, everyone knew the Westmorelands would want to stay together. Besides," he said, chuckling, "no one around our parts wanted to be responsible for Bane."

"Bane?"

"Yes. It's short for Brisbane. He's my youngest brother who likes his share of mischief. He was only eight when my parents were killed and he took their deaths pretty hard."

"How old is he now?"

"Twenty-two and still hot under the collar in more ways than one. I wish there was something holding his interest these days other than a certain female in Denver."

Pam nodded. She couldn't help but wonder if there

was a certain female in Denver holding Dillon's interest, as well.

"Do all of you still live close to one another?" she asked.

"Yes, Great-Grandpa Raphel purchased a lot of land back in the thirties. When each Westmoreland reaches the age of twenty-five they are given a hundred-acre tract of land, which is why we all live in close proximity to each other. As the oldest cousin, I inherited the family home where everyone seems to congregate most of the time."

He then asked her, "How old were you when your great-grandfather passed?"

"He died before I was born, but I heard a lot about him. What about Raphel? How old were you when he passed?"

"He died before I was born, too. My great-grandmother lived until I was two, so I don't rightly remember much of her, either. But I do remember my grandparents, Grampa Stern and Gramma Paula. It was Grampa Stern who used to tell us stories about Raphel, but never did he mention anything about past wives or other siblings. In fact, he claimed Raphel had been an only child. That makes me wonder how much he truly knew about his own father."

Pam paused for a moment and then said, "I guess there are secrets in most families."

"Yes, like Raphel running off with the preacher's wife," he said.

"And you think Raphel eventually married her?"

"Not sure of that, either," Dillon replied. "Since she was legally married to the preacher, I don't see how a marriage between them could take place, which is why I'm curious as to what happened to her once they fled Georgia."

"But her name, as well as Portia's, are shown as former wives on documents you've found?" she asked, trying to get a greater understanding of just what kind of life his great-grandfather may have led.

"Two of my Atlanta cousins, Quade and Cole, own a security firm and they did a background check, going as far back as the early nineteen-hundreds. Old land deeds were discovered for Raphel and they list four separate women as his wives. So far we know two of them—the preacher's wife and Portia Novak—were already legally married. We can only assume Raphel lived with them pretending to be married."

He paused a moment and then glanced around and asked, "Do you come up here often?"

His question made her realize they had been standing still long enough and were awfully close, so she shifted toward the attic door. "Not as often as I used to. I just moved back to Gamble last year when my father passed. Like you, I'm the oldest and I wanted to care for my sisters. I am their legal guardian."

Dillon nodded and stepped back when she opened the attic door. He had noticed the way she had interacted with her sisters last night at dinner. It was obvious they were close.

"That's my great-grandfather's trunk over there. It's my understanding that he and your great-grandfather were partners in a dairy business, which was very profitable at the time. I know there are a lot of business records in there, as well as some of Raphel's belongings. It seems he made a quick getaway when he left Gamble."

Dillon shot her a glance. "You have some of Raphel's belongings?"

"Yes," she said, moving toward the trunk. "I didn't mention it at dinner last night."

He understood the reason she hadn't done so. Her fiancé probably would have had something to say about it. It was quite obvious the man could make an argument out of just about any subject.

Instead of immediately following her over to the trunk, Dillon stood back for a moment and watched her go. His gaze was focused on her. The possibility that some of his great-grandfather's belongings might be inside that trunk intrigued him. But she intrigued him more.

She was wearing jeans and a pretty pink blouse that added an ultrafeminine touch. He couldn't help but notice the seductive curves outlined in those jeans. Walking behind her up the stairs to the attic had been hell. He was certain sweat had popped out on his brow with every step she'd taken.

When she saw he hadn't followed her, she turned and slanted him a glance. "Are you all right?"

No, he wasn't all right. One part of his brain was trying to convince him that, although she was an engaged woman, she wasn't married yet, so she was still available. But another part of him, the one looking at the ring on her finger, knew to make a pass in any way would be crossing a line. But hell, he was tempted.

She held his gaze, and he realized at that moment he hadn't given her an answer. "Yes, I'm fine. Just overwhelmed." If only she knew how much and the reason why.

"I understand how you feel. What you said last night at dinner is true for me, as well. I consider family important. Although you never knew him, you want to know as much about your great-grandfather as you can learn. I think it is admirable that you want to do so."

She glanced down at the trunk and then back at him. "I just hope you don't think you're going to find out everything there is to know about your great-grandfather in one day, Dillon. Even after I open that trunk it might spur you to ask more questions, seek more answers."

"And if I need to come back here?" he asked, knowing she knew where he was going with the question.

"You're welcome to come back for as long as it takes."

His gaze held hers intensely as he asked, "Will Fletcher be okay with it? Like I said earlier, I don't want to cause any problems between the two of you."

"There won't be any problems. Now, aren't you going to open this trunk? I've been dying to do so for years, but growing up we were always told it was off limits." Her lips curved at the corners. "But I will admit to defying orders once and poking around in there. At that time, I didn't see anything that held my interest."

Dillon smiled as he crossed the floor toward her. Like his at home, the attic here was huge. As a boy, the attic had been one of his favorite places to hide when he wanted some alone time. This room was full of boxes and trunks, but they had been arranged in a neat order, nothing like the way his attic looked back home. And there was that lone, small rectangular window that allowed just enough sunlight to shine through.

Kneeling, he pulled off a key that was taped on the side of the trunk and began working at the lock. Moments later he lifted open the lid. There were a lot of papers, business books, a couple of work shirts that had aged with time, a bottle of wine, a compass and a tattered looking journal.

He glanced up at Pam. "Mind if I take a look at this?"

"No, I don't mind. In fact, there's a letter inside."

He lifted a brow as he opened the journal and, sure enough, a letter whose envelope had turned yellow, lay on the front page. The name on the envelope was still legible. It simply said *Westmoreland*. He glanced back over at her.

"Like I said, although the trunk was off limits, I couldn't help but snoop that one time. That's how I knew about that letter."

Dillon couldn't hide his smile as he opened the sealed letter. It read, *"Whomever comes to get Raphel's belongings just needs to know that he was a good and decent man and I don't blame him for leaving and taking Portia with him."*

It had been signed by Pam's great-grandfather Jay. Dillon put the letter back in the envelope and glanced up at Pam. "This is all very confusing. Think you can shed some light on it?"

She shook her head. "No, sorry. For a man not to hold

any animosity against the man that took his wife is strange. Perhaps Raphel did Jay a favor if he didn't want to be married to her anyway. But that theory is really stretching it a bit. A man's wife is a man's wife, and Portia had been Jay's wife."

"And what about Lila Elms?"

She shrugged. "I can't tell you anything about her, other than they must have parted ways between Atlanta and here, because from all I've heard when Raphel arrived in Gamble he was a single man."

She glanced at her watch. "There are a few phone calls that I need to make, so I'm going to leave you for a while. Take as much time as you like up here, and if you need me for any reason, I'll be downstairs in the kitchen."

"All right."

She moved toward the attic door.

"Pamela?"

She glanced back around. "Yes?"

He smiled. "Thanks."

She smiled back. "Don't mention it."

Dillon released a deep breath the moment Pam left, closing the attic door behind her. Pamela Novak was a temptation he had best leave alone. All the while she had been in this room, he had tried keeping the conversation going, anything to suppress the desires that had run rampant through him.

What was there about her that ruffled his senses every time she was within ten feet of him? What was there about her that made a number of unnamed and undefined sensations run through him? It had been hard as hell to maintain his composure and control around her.

Perhaps his dilemma had to do with her understanding of his need to delve into his family's history, his desire to know as much about Raphel Westmoreland as he could find out. Even some of his siblings and cousins didn't understand what was driving him, although they did support him. He appreciated them for it, but support and understanding were two different things.

However, he had a gut feeling Pamela did understand. She not only understood but was willing to help him any way she could...even if it meant stirring her fiancé's ire.

Deciding he needed to do what he'd come to Gamble to do, he pulled a chair out of a corner and placed it in front of the trunk. Picking up Jay Novak's journal, he began reading.

Four

Pam glanced at the clock on the kitchen wall. Dillon had been up in the attic for over an hour, and she couldn't help but wonder how things were going. More than once she'd thought about going up to find out but had talked herself out of it. Instead she got busy looking over scripts for new plays her students had submitted.

The ringing of her phone interrupted her thoughts and she had a feeling who the caller was without bothering to look at caller ID. Sighing deeply, she picked up the phone. "Hello?"

"How are you, Pamela? This is Fletcher."

"I'm fine, Fletcher. How are things in Laramie?"

"They are fine, but I received a call and I'm going to have to leave here and go to Montana and check on a store there. A massive snowstorm caused a power failure that lasted a couple of days, and a lot of our refrigerated items were destroyed."

"I'm sorry to hear that."

"So am I. That means I'll be flying to Montana to meet with the insurance company representative. It may take a few days and I might not be back until the end of the week."

She could lie and say she was sorry to hear that, but she really wasn't. She had felt the two of them needed space and this was a way she could get it. Since agreeing to marry him, he'd made it a point to see her practically every day.

"You can make me happy and come spend some time with me here." His words intruded into her thoughts. The two of them hadn't slept together. Although he had brought up the idea several times, she had avoided the issue with him.

"Thanks for the invite, but I have a lot to do here. Besides, I need to be here for my sisters."

She didn't have to see him to know his jaw was probably tight from anger right now. This was not the first time he had tried to talk her into going out of town with him since they'd become engaged.

He didn't say anything for a moment and when he did speak again, she was not surprised by his change in subject. "And where is Westmoreland? Did he show up today?"

She had no reason to lie. "Yes, he showed up. In fact, he's still here, upstairs in the attic going through some things."

"Why couldn't he take the stuff with him and go through it back at the hotel?"

Fletcher's tone, as well as his words, annoyed her. "I saw no reason for him to take anything back to the hotel. I regret you evidently have a problem with it."

"I'm just looking out for you, Pamela," he said after a brief pause. "I still feel you don't know the man well enough to be there alone with him."

"Then I guess you just need to chalk it up as bad judgment on my part. Goodbye, Fletcher."

Without waiting for him to say anything else, she hung up the phone. He would fume for a few hours and then he would call her back later and apologize once he realized just how controlling he'd acted.

Pam eased back to the table and picked up the papers once again, determined to tuck Fletcher and his attitude away until later. She had agreed to marry him and she *would* marry him, since her sisters' futures and not losing her family home meant everything to her.

Dillon closed the journal and stood to stretch his legs. He was used to being dressed in a business suit every day, instead of casual jeans and a shirt. That morning he had checked in with Ted Boston, his business manager, to see how things were going at his real estate firm and, not surprisingly, Ted had everything under control. He had made his firm into a billion-dollar company with hard work and by hiring the right people to work for him.

He glanced at his watch, finding it hard to believe that

two hours had passed already. He looked down at the journal. At least part of his curiosity had been satisfied as to what had happened to Lila, the wife of the preacher from Georgia.

According to what Raphel had shared with Jay, the old preacher had been abusing his young wife. Church members had turned their heads with the mind-set that what went on behind a married couple's closed doors was their business, especially when it involved a preacher.

Evidently, Raphel hadn't seen it that way. He had come up with a plan to rescue Lila from the clutches of the abusive preacher—a plan his family had not supported. After taking Lila as far away as Texas, Raphel had helped her get established in the small Texas town of Copperhead, on the outskirts of Austin. Raphel had been her protector, never her lover, and before moving on he had purchased a small tract of land and given it to her to make a new beginning for herself.

Dillon smiled, thinking, at least in the case of Lila, Raphel had been a wife saver and not a wife stealer. Given the woman's situation, Dillon figured he would have done the same thing. He'd discovered that when it came to the opposite sex, Westmoreland men had this ingrained sense of protection. He just regretted that Raphel had severed ties with his family.

At that moment Dillon's stomach started to growl, reminding him that he hadn't eaten anything since early that morning and it was afternoon already. It was time for him to head back over to the hotel.

* * *

Pam had been intensely involved in reading one of her students' scripts when suddenly she felt sensations curl inside her stomach at the same time chill bumps began to form on her arms.

She glanced up and met Dillon's gaze as he stepped into the kitchen. She wondered how her body had known of his presence before her mind. And why even now the sensations curling her stomach had intensified. She decided to speak before he had a chance to do so, not sure what havoc the sensations combined with his deep, disturbingly sexy voice would play on her senses.

"How did things go? Did you discover anything about your great-grandfather that you didn't know before?" she asked, hoping he didn't hear the strain in her voice.

He smiled, and the effect of that smile was just as bad as if he'd spoken. He had a dimpled smile that showed beautiful white teeth. "Yes. At least, thanks to your great-grandfather's journal, I was able to solve the mystery of Lila, woman number one."

"Did they eventually marry?" she asked, curiously.

"No, from what I read, Lila's preacher husband was an abusive man and Lila sought out Raphel's help to escape the situation. He took her as far as Copperhead, Texas, hung around while she got on her feet, established her with a new identity and then moved on."

Pam nodded. "That explains why he wasn't married when he arrived here in Gamble."

"Yes, but it doesn't explain why he would run off with your great-grandfather's wife. And so far nothing

I've read explains it, but then I didn't get through the entire journal. Not even halfway. Jay would digress and talk about the dairy business and how it was doing. But from what I've read so far, it seemed that he and Raphel were close, which doesn't explain how my great-grandfather could betray him the way he did."

Pam didn't say anything for a moment and then she asked, "So, are you taking a break before reading some more?"

"No, it's getting late and I think it won't be a good idea to be here when your fiancé arrives this evening. I've outstayed my welcome today anyway, and I appreciate you giving me a chance to read the journal."

"You're welcome." And before she could think better of her actions, she said, "And I'd like to invite you to stay for dinner. I'm sure my sisters would love hearing what you've discovered today. I think you piqued their interest at dinner yesterday and they see this as some sort of family mystery needing to be solved. At some time or another everyone has heard about Raphel Westmoreland and how he ran off with my great-grandfather's first wife."

Dillon leaned against the kitchen cabinet. "I'm surprised no one in your family has been curious enough to find out what really happened."

Pam shrugged. "I guess you have to understand how some women think, namely my great-grandmother. I'm sure she could have cared less why her predecessor ran off with another man, and the less the family talked about Portia, the better."

She tilted her head and looked up at him. "So will you take me up on my invitation and stay for dinner?"

Pam's words intruded into his thoughts and he looked up and over at her, holding her gaze a moment. "And what about Fletcher? How is he going to handle me sitting at your dinner table two evenings in a row?"

He watched as she nervously bit her bottom lip and then lifted her chin. "There's nothing wrong with me inviting someone I consider a family friend to dinner. Besides, Fletcher is out of town for a few days."

He nodded, considered her words and decided not to read anything into them. It was an invitation to dinner, nothing more. As long as he remembered she was an engaged woman, everything would be all right.

Only problem with that was that the more he saw her, and the more he was around her, the more he was attracted to her. And the more he was attracted to her, the more he could admit, whether it was honorable or not, that he wanted her.

He swallowed and intentionally glanced out the window, needing to break eye contact with Pam. What he'd just inwardly admitted wasn't good, but he was being honest with himself. That meant as soon as he could find out all the answers he wanted about Raphel, he hoped in the next couple of days, he would return home.

He glanced back at her, met her gaze, felt the pull, the attraction, and although she might never admit it to anyone, not even to herself, he knew it was mutual. He knew he should ask if he could take the journal back to the hotel and spend the next several days reading it, out of such close proximity to her and this unusual sexual chemistry he felt whenever they were near each other.

But for some reason he couldn't. "If you're sure it will be okay then, yes, I'd love to join you and your sisters for dinner."

"And you're sure he's coming back for dinner, Pammie?" Nadia asked with excitement in her voice as she helped her oldest sister set the table.

Pam lifted a brow. She couldn't remember the last time Nadia or Paige had gotten excited about someone coming for dinner, least of all a man. The first time she had invited Fletcher, they had almost boycotted dinner until she'd had a good, hard talk about being courteous and displaying Novak manners.

"Yes, he said he was going back to the hotel to change clothes and would be coming back."

"And don't you think he's very handsome, Pam?" Paige chimed in to ask.

Pam turned after placing the last plate on the table and faced her three sisters. Although Jill hadn't voiced her excitement, Pam knew it was there—she could clearly see it on her face. The one thing she didn't want her sisters to think was that Dillon's presence at dinner had anything to do with her engagement to Fletcher. She knew what they were trying to do, and it was time she made sure they understood that it wasn't working.

"Yes, he is handsome, Paige, but so is Fletcher. But I'm not marrying a man because of his looks. I'm not that vain and I hope the three of you aren't, either. To set the record straight, so the three of you fully know that what you're doing isn't working, I *will* be marrying Fletcher."

Jill smiled. "We have no idea what you're talking about, Pam."

Pam rolled her eyes and was about to give them a good talking-to when the sound of the doorbell stopped her. "Okay, that's our guest and I want you on your best behavior, and please keep in mind that I am engaged to marry Fletcher."

Jill made a face and then said, "Please, don't remind us."

"We're glad you found out something about your great-grandfather today, Dillon," Nadia said, smiling.

Dillon couldn't help but return her smile, thinking she reminded him a lot of his cousin Bailey when she'd been Nadia's age. There was an innocence about her, while at the same time if you looked into her eyes long enough, there was mischief there, as well. The same thing could be said about Paige, but Jill was a different story.

There was something about her and her antics tonight that reminded him of Bane. The thought of a female Bane made him cringe more than a little. Her eyes twinkled when she encouraged him to talk about his family. He couldn't help but wonder if she was truly interested, or if her inquisition was a ploy. And he was smart enough to figure out it all came back to the same thing as last night. For some reason Pam's sisters were not happy with the man she had chosen to marry. It didn't take a rocket scientist to see that.

"Would you like something more to eat, Dillon?"

He glanced over at Pam. Their gazes met across the table and he smiled while at the same time fought down the tightening of his gut. He'd never been a man easily distracted by a beautiful face, but in the last forty-eight hours he'd known the real experience of feeling weak in the knees and having his heart thud mercilessly in his chest.

"No, and I appreciate your invitation to dinner."

"Tell us some more about Bane. He sounds like someone I'd like to meet one day," Jill said.

"No, he's not," both Dillon and Pam said simultaneously, and then they couldn't help but glance across the table at each other and laugh. They agreed with each other on that point.

Pam excused herself to go get dessert, a chocolate cake she had baked earlier. Dillon smiled at the three females staring at him and, as soon as Pam left the room, he was surprised when they lit into him with questions they dared not ask while their older sister was still in the room.

Nadia went first. Her dark eyes, as beautiful as her older sister's, stared him down. "Do you think Pammie is pretty?"

He smiled. That was easy enough for him to answer and do so truthfully. "Yes, she's pretty."

"Do you have a girlfriend?" Paige quickly asked.

He chuckled. "No, I don't have a girlfriend."

"Would you be interested in Pam if she wasn't engaged?"

Jill's question would have shocked the hell out of him if he hadn't gotten used to her tactics by now. She shot straight from the hip and he intended to answer her the same way.

"The key point to remember is that your sister *is* engaged, so whether I would be interested is a moot point, now, isn't it? But to answer your question, my answer would be yes, I would be interested."

"Interested in what?" Pam asked, returning and toting a plate with a huge chocolate cake.

"Nothing," three voices said at once.

Pam lifted a brow as she glanced at her sisters. She then looked over at Dillon and he couldn't help but smile and shrug his shoulders. Joining Pam and her sisters for dinner made him feel right at home and he wasn't sure that was a good thing.

"I think I need to apologize for anything my sisters might have said that could have grated on your nerves tonight," Pam said, walking Dillon out to his car. She had convinced herself this would be the only way she could get a few private words in without her sisters' ears perking at each and every word.

He chuckled. "Hey, it wasn't bad. I enjoyed their company. Yours, too. And dinner was wonderful."

"Thanks."

They didn't say anything for a few moments and then she asked, "Will you be coming back tomorrow? To continue reading Jay's journal?"

When they came to his car he leaned against it to face her. "Only if you say it's okay. I don't want to wear out my welcome."

She chuckled. "You won't be. Besides, finding out more about Raphel and Portia is like a puzzle waiting to be pieced together."

Pam knew she probably should suggest that he take the journal with him—that way he wouldn't have to bother coming back tomorrow—but for some reason she couldn't do that.

"Well, I guess I'd better let you go now. See you tomorrow," she said, backing up, putting proper distance between them.

"Good night," he said.

Dillon opened the door and got into the car but sat there until Pam had raced up the stairs, let herself inside and closed the door behind her. He saw three pairs of curtains automatically fall back into place in upstairs windows, and couldn't help but chuckle at the notion that he and Pam had been spied on. To be honest, he wasn't surprised.

As he drove off, he could only shake his head when he remembered his siblings' and cousins' reaction to Tammi when he'd brought her home, a year before they'd married. Although his parents and aunt and uncle had tried making the Westmoreland clan behave, it had been pretty obvious that Tammi hadn't been too well received. But that hadn't stopped him for marrying her the following year and bringing her home as his wife. Now he wished that it had.

He shifted in his seat to pull his cell phone out of his jeans pocket, hoping tonight he could pick up a signal. He smiled when he did and immediately placed a call home.

Ramsey answered on the second ring. "The West-morelands."

"Hey, Ram, it's Dillon. How are things going?"

"As well as can be expected. Bane's been behaving, so that's good."

Yes, that was good, Dillon thought.

"I went up to the big house and got all your mail," Ramsey was saying.

"Thanks."

"You find out anything on Raphel yet?" Ramsey asked.

"Yes." Dillon then spent the next half hour bringing his cousin up to date on what he'd uncovered that day from Jay's journal.

"And Jay Novak's great-granddaughter is actually nice to you? After Raphel ran off with her great-grandfather's wife?"

Dillon chuckled. "Yes, she's operating on the premise of good riddance. If Portia hadn't left then Jay would never have met and married her great-grand-mother. Needless to say, Pam has no problem with Raphel running off with the woman."

"Pam?"

Dillon heard the curiosity in Ramsey's voice and knew why. Ramsey of all people knew how hard it had been in making the real estate firm he had inherited from his father and uncle into the billion-dollar com-pany it was today, taking care of the Westmoreland stronghold and being responsible for all those West-morelands who were still dependent while they were away at college.

"Yes, Pam is her name, and before you ask, the answer again is yes, she is beautiful. The most beautiful woman I've ever set eyes on."

And before Ramsey could say anything, he quickly added, "And she's engaged."

"Umm, have you met her fiancé?" Ramsey wanted to know.

"Yes, and he's an ass."

Ramsey chuckled. "How did a beautiful woman get engaged to an ass?"

"Beats me and it's none of my business."

"That's the difference between me and you, cuz. I would make it my business, especially if she was the most beautiful woman I'd ever seen. You know what they say about it not being over until the fat lady sings? Well, in this case, she's not off limits until the wedding is over."

"That's not my style, Ram."

"Typically, it's not mine, either, being the loner that I am, but I've learned that with some things you need to know when and how to adjust your thinking, be flexible and restructure your thought process. Especially if it's a woman you want."

Dillon blinked, taken aback by Ramsey's statement. "What makes you think she's a woman I want?"

"I can hear it in your voice. Do you deny it?"

Dillon opened his mouth to do that very thing and then closed his mouth shut. No, he couldn't deny it, because his cousin who knew him so well had just spoken the truth. And the question of the hour was whether or not he intended to do anything about it.

Five

Pam was trying, desperately so, to convince herself that the only reason she was sitting at the kitchen table and staring out the window was to study all the Indian paint-brushes that were still blooming this late in the year.

It wasn't working.

Just like it wasn't working to try and convince herself the only reason she'd gone to bed with thoughts of Dillon on her mind instead of the man she was engaged to marry was because Dillon had been to dinner the last couple of nights. The reason that argument wouldn't hold up was because, although Fletcher had been dropping in for dinner quite often, she had yet to take visions of him to her bed. She had yet to remember, in vivid detail, what he'd been wearing the last time she'd seen him, and yet to hear the sound of his voice in her head in the wee hours of the morning.

So why was Dillon Westmoreland causing so much havoc in her life when she should be concentrating on setting the best date to marry Fletcher? The main thing that had been nagging at her since meeting Dillon was the fact that he could arouse feelings and sensations within her that Fletcher didn't. Was that something she should be concerned about, she wondered.

She quickly decided that it didn't really matter if she should be concerned, since Fletcher was the only one capable of getting her out of such a dismal situation. Their marriage would not be one of love and, the way things were looking, it wouldn't be one of passion either. But she would make do. She really didn't have a choice.

The ringing of the phone intruded her thoughts. Getting up from the table she quickly crossed the room to pick it up, but turned to make sure she still had a good view out the window. "Hello."

"I called to see if you've come to your senses and called off your engagement."

Pam couldn't do anything, but shake her head and smile. She wasn't sure who was worse, her sisters or her best friend from college, Iris Michaels. From Iris's initial meeting with Fletcher, he had rubbed her the wrong way and she hadn't gotten over it yet. "No, sorry, the wedding is still on, so I hope you haven't forgotten your promise to be my maid of honor."

Pam could picture Iris sitting behind the desk of the PR company she owned in Los Angeles with a beautiful view of the Pacific. Iris would be tapping a pen either on her desk or to the side of her face, trying to think of a way to get out of the promise she'd made their second year in college together over a peanut butter and jelly sandwich. Their days in college had been hard. Money had been tight, so they had made do, shared practically everything and had become best friends for life.

Right out of college, Iris had met, fallen in love with and married Garlan Knight. Garlan, a stuntman, had been killed while working on a major film less than a year into their marriage. That was four years ago and, although Iris dated on occasion, she had long ago proclaimed that she would never give her heart to another man because the pain of losing the person she loved wasn't worth it.

"I'm trying to forget I made that promise. So what's been going on with you lately?"

At first Pam couldn't decide whether she should mention anything about Dillon and then thought, why not? Chances were, when Iris came to visit, her sisters would tell her about him anyway, and then Iris would accuse her of holding secrets. "Well, there is something I need to tell you about. I had a visitor this week."

While periodically glancing out the window, Pam told Iris how Dillon had shown up two nights ago. Surprisingly, Iris didn't ask a lot of questions; she listened attentively, giving Pam the chance to finish. "So, there you have it," Pam finally said, glad it was over and done with. She made an attempt to move to another subject—about how things were going at the drama school—when Iris stopped her.

"Hey, not so fast, Pam. What aren't you telling me?"

Pam rolled her eyes. "I've told you everything."

"Then why did you deliberately leave out any details about how this guy looks? You know I'm a visual person."

Pam breathed in deeply. "He's good-looking."

"How good-looking?"

"Very good-looking, Iris," she said, hoping that would be the end of it.

"On a scale of one to ten with ten being the sexiest, how would you rate him?" Iris asked.

"Why do you want to know?"

"Just answer the question, please," Iris demanded.

When Pam didn't say anything for a moment, deciding to keep her lips sealed, Iris said, "I'm waiting."

Pam rolled her eyes again and then said, "Okay, he a ten."

"A ten?"

"Yes, Iris, a ten. He is so darn pleasing to the eyes it's a shame," she said, inwardly blaming Iris for making her tell all.

"What about his personality?"

Pam thought about how dinner had gone yesterday and how pleasant it had been for her sisters to feel included in the dinner discussions. Dillon had held their focus because he had paid attention to them, as if what they had to say was important, not trivial like Fletcher would often do. Yes, she would have to say he had a nice personality.

"He's nice, Iris, and his personality goes right along with it."

"Would he be someone that would interest you if you weren't engaged to Fletcher?"

Pam frowned. "Why would you ask me something like that when I *am* engaged to Fletcher?"

"Cut all the drama, Pam, and answer the question."

Pam's frown deepened because she knew the answer to Iris's question without thinking much about it. "Yes, he would be. In a heartbeat." And then because she had to tell someone and Iris, being her best friend, was the likely candidate, she said, "I'm attracted to him. Isn't that awful?"

"Why is it awful? You and I both know why you're marrying Fletcher, which I still think is a mistake. I refuse to believe there is not a bank anywhere that will loan you the money you need to pay off that second mortgage."

"We're talking about a million dollars, Iris. You know how much hassle you got from the banks when you wanted to borrow half that much to start your PR business. I have very little in savings and what I do have Jill will need for college next year. And Paige and Nadia need a home. I can't expect them to move away from the only home they've known. A home that's been in the Novak family for over a hundred years." Pam sighed in frustration. "I still can't believe Dad didn't take all that into consideration when he took out that second mortgage."

"If Fletcher was really a nice guy, he would cosign for you to get that money without any strings attached," Iris said. "For him to put stipulations on his help by asking you to marry him is just downright underhanded, if you ask me."

Pam didn't say anything since she had heard it all from Iris before, several times. When Iris finally ended her spiel, Pam said, "Marrying Fletcher won't be so bad, Iris."

"It will be if you're sentencing yourself to a life without love and passion, and we both know that you are. I loved Garlan and the passion we shared was wonderful. I can't imagine being married to a man I didn't love or who didn't do anything for me sexually."

Pam was silent for a moment and then said quietly, "Well, I can. I don't have a choice, Iris."

For a short while Iris didn't say anything, either. "Then maybe now is the time to enjoy passion while you can."

Pam blinked. "Just what are you suggesting?"

"You've admitted you're attracted to Dillon Westmoreland, so take advantage of that attraction and think about yourself for a change, not the house or the land or your sisters. Think about Pamela."

"I can't do that," Pam said.

"Sure you can. Are you going to deny you haven't been thinking about Dillon Westmoreland in the wee hours of the night?"

Pam almost dropped the phone. "How did you know?"

Iris laughed. "Hey, you said the man is a ten. Men who are tens can't help but find their way into a woman's nightly dreams, regardless of whether she's single, engaged or married. It happens. My advice to you is to bring him out of your dreams into your reality. You will be married to Fletcher until death do you part. Do you want to go through the next fifty, sixty or seventy years without feeling any passion again?"

"I told you about my past experiences with passion, Iris," she said, remembering the couple of times she had slept with guys and the disappointment she'd felt afterward. She hadn't heard the bells and whistles, nor had she felt any earthquakes like Iris had claimed she would.

"That's why you owe it to yourself to try things out one more time. I bet Mr. Ten will deliver."

At that moment Pam saw Dillon's car pull into her yard. Moments later she watched him get out. Today he was wearing a pair of khakis and a dark green shirt. And just like yesterday and the day before, he looked handsome and utterly sexy.

Her gaze scanned over his body and, as if he knew she was staring out the window, he turned and looked directly toward her. She immediately felt heat suffuse her body at the same time blood gushed through her veins. Yes, there was no doubt in her mind that if given the chance he could deliver.

"Pam?"

"Yes?"

"When will you be seeing him again?"

Pam licked her lips as she continued to stare. Dillon hadn't moved. He was still standing in that same spot gazing through the window. He couldn't see her, although she could see him. Yet it was as if he knew she was there, knew he was holding her attention. She wondered if he had any clue about the thoughts flowing through her mind at that particular moment. If he did, he would probably jump back into the car and hightail it off her property.

"Pam?"

"I see him now, Iris. Through the kitchen window. He just drove up and has gotten out the car."

"Then the ball is now in your court, Pam. And you owe it to yourself to play it."

Dillon leaned back against his car as he stared into what he knew was Pam's secret window. Somehow he knew she was there, looking at him, with the same intensity with which he was looking at her.

Ramsey's words of last night rang in his ears, and the thought of wanting her made his breathing quicken and his guts clench. If she knew what he was thinking she probably wouldn't let him within a foot of her, and definitely not inside her house.

He had soaked in the bathtub in his hotel room last night with his eyes closed and thought about her. He had gone to bed thinking about her. And he had awakened that morning thinking about her. A woman who belonged to another man.

Not yet though, as Ramsey had pointed out to him last night.

He would be out of line to make a pass at her, so he wouldn't. But he intended to do everything to incite her to make a pass at him…if she was interested. If she wasn't, then he knew he would have to control his urges. But if she *was* interested, then those urges would be set free.

There was a chance that he was reading too much into the looks they had exchanged across the dinner table last night, or the heat that he'd felt. But there was only one way to find out. If she decided to indulge in this thing he felt between them, then that meant her relationship with Fletcher wasn't as tight as it needed to be.

Deciding he couldn't stay outside and stare into the window for the rest of the day, he drew in a deep breath before shifting his eyes away to move toward her front door. He took his time walking up the steps and by the time he lifted his hand to knock, the door had opened and she stood there.

His guts clenched harder as he lowered his hand to his side. She looked as beautiful as usual, but today she was wearing her hair differently. It appeared fluffed up and it billowed around her shoulders like she had used one of those curling irons on it.

His gaze moved from her head to her eyes and saw her watching him as intently as he was watching her. He then moved his gaze lower to her lips. They were the same lips he had dreamed about last night. Many times.

Then his eyes followed the hand that she nervously ran down her throat to the V of her knit top. He couldn't help but notice how her breasts swelled in perfect formation against the blouse.

"I've been waiting for you," she said, snagging his attention as his gaze shifted back to her face. Captured her eyes.

"I know," he said in a voice that sounded husky to his own ears.

He didn't think he needed to explain. For some reason he sensed that she fully understood. "Am I allowed in today?" he asked as a smile touched his lips. She had yet to move from in front of the door.

She blinked as if she'd just realized that fact. "Oops. Sorry about that. Yes, please come in," she said before stepping aside.

He strolled past her, took a whiff of her scent and felt his entire body respond. Instantly. Why was the sexual chemistry between them stronger today than yesterday? More potent. Today, they seemed to be on instinct, with little or no control.

When she closed the door behind her and leaned back against it, she eyed him warily. He didn't say anything for a while. "And how are you doing today, Pam?"

"I'm doing fine," she said, in what sounded like a strained voice. "What about you?"

"I'm doing okay," he said. No need to tell her about his restless night, in which he had dreamed endlessly of her and all the things he wouldn't mind doing to her.

"I guess you're eager to get back to reading that journal."

He chuckled. He was eager all right, but that journal wasn't what was driving his eagerness. "Sort of."

Again he wasn't entirely sure just what was going on between them. What had happened since yesterday to make them so sexually charged that the very air they were breathing sizzled. He pulled in a deep breath, both feeling it and fighting it.

"I'm going up to the attic now," he said in a low voice, just loud enough for her to hear. "You probably have a lot to do, so forget that I'm here."

She smiled in a way that sent blood rushing all through him. "I doubt I'll be able to do that."

"Do what?" he asked.

She held his gaze. "Forget that you're here."

He wanted to ask why, but decided not to do so. She was the one who was engaged. If any boundaries were going to be crossed, she would have to be the one to take the first step over. "You can try," he suggested.

"And if I can't?" she asked in a somewhat shaky tone.

Holding her gaze, he breathed in and pulled more sexually charged air into his lungs. He felt it stirring in his chest and flowing in his extremities, causing the lower part of him to harden. Throb. He even felt a sheen of sweat form on his brow, which compelled him to say, "Then you know where I am."

Without saying anything else, he turned and headed slowly up the stairs to the attic.

Pam leaned against the door and watched as Dillon disappeared up the stairs before releasing the breath she'd been holding. She was too shaken to think straight, and too tempted to follow him up those stairs to move away from the door.

She glanced down at the ring on her finger, the ring Fletcher had placed there. Instead of feeling guilt, she felt desperation as Iris's words rang loud in her ears. *"Then the ball is now in your court, Pam. And you owe it to yourself to play it."*

If only Iris knew just how much she wanted to play it. Maybe her best friend did know, which was why she'd

said what she had. Iris did know love and she understood
passion. She had been happy with Garlan and when
Garlan had been taken away from her so suddenly and
unexpectedly, Iris's life had nearly fallen apart.

She had been there for Iris, to encourage her to go
on with life, and now Iris was there for her, encourag-
ing her to do something for herself before it was too late.
Before she legally became Mrs. Fletcher Mallard.

But still, she needed to pull herself together and
wondered why she would even consider following her
impulses with a man she'd met only three days ago.
What was there about Dillon that drew her to him, made
her feel things she'd never felt before? Made her desire
things she'd never before wanted?

Something you'd tried twice and left you disappointed.

Why did she think with him it would be different?
Why did a part deep inside of her know that it would?
It might be the way he looked at her, the heated intensity she felt from his gaze, the desire she saw even
without him speaking a single word.

Those were the things that were urging her to move
away from the door and propelling her to walk up the
stairs, one step at a time.

Dillon stared at the words written in the journal, his
eyes feeling the strain of seeing the words but not com-
prehending them. He had read the same sentence three
times, but his mind was not on what Jay Novak had
written close to a century ago. Instead his mind was on
the woman he had left downstairs.

Why did some things have to be so complicated? Why had the Novaks' homestead been the first place on his list in his quest to find the key to his heritage as the eldest son of the Denver Westmorelands? And why was he lusting after a woman who another man had already claimed?

Dillon closed the journal and rubbed his hand down his face. Fletcher Mallard was a successful businessman and probably a prime catch for any woman in these parts. Evidently there was something about the man Pam had found to her liking.

And there was evidently something about him that she'd also found lacking.

No matter how things appeared, and regardless of the fact he'd only known her for three days, he refused to believe, or even consider the possibility that Pamela Novak was the type of woman who could love one man and mess around with another. So he could only come to the conclusion that she was not in love with Fletcher. Then why was she marrying him, Dillon wondered.

Wealth? Prestige? Security?

It hadn't been hard to figure out that Tammi had only been interested in him because he had made the pros, and the thought of being the wife of a professional basketball player had stroked her fancy. When he had given it all up, had walked away to handle his family's business, he'd known she assumed it was only short term, although he'd always told her differently. When she couldn't get him to walk away from family obligations, she had left.

Dillon's thoughts were interrupted by the soft sound

of footsteps approaching. He felt a quick tightness in his stomach. His entire being tensed in anticipation, knowing it could be only one person. He could no longer sit, so he stood and had placed the journal aside by the time Pam crossed the threshold.

His heart began beating wildly in his chest and his body automatically hardened at the sight of her standing there. She had come to him. He hadn't been certain that she would, but she had.

His gaze scanned her body. He had meant to tell her earlier that he thought the outfit she was wearing, a white blouse and a dark blue skirt, looked good on her. It had been the first time he'd seen her legs and they were definitely a beautiful pair.

"Looks like it might rain later," she said. She strolled over to the window to glance out. While she looked out the window, he was looking at her. The sun was still shining so he wondered how she figured it might rain later. If anything, he figured it might snow. Like Denver, Gamble had its sunny days and cold nights, especially this time of the year. But at the moment he didn't care about either. The only thing on his mind right now was Pam.

She glanced over at him and he realized he hadn't responded to her earlier comment about the weather. "Yes, it just might rain," he said quietly.

She nodded and turned back to the window. His throat had started to go dry, while at the same time liquid fire raced through his veins. At that moment he decided she had made the first move and now it was time to make his.

Helplessly and with an urgency he felt all the way to the bottom of his feet, he slowly crossed the room, knowing each step was taking him closer to the woman he wanted. When he came to a stop behind her, she turned and looked up at him.

He gazed down into her face thinking she looked uncertain and indecisive. "You give. I take. No regrets," he said in a thick voice.

Dillon hoped she understood because he meant every word. She glanced down at the engagement ring on her hand and his gaze followed hers. And while he watched, she twisted the ring off her finger and then placed it on the windowsill.

Then she looked up, met his gaze and said in a soft, barely audible voice the exact same words he'd spoken to her. "You give. I take. No regrets."

Her words touched an inner coil within him, made desire drum through his entire body at a pace that had him breathing in deeply.

He took another step toward her and heard himself groan low in his throat at the same moment he reached out and pulled her into his arms. And with a hunger that he felt all the way to his toes, he lowered his mouth as she parted her lips. The connection was explosive, and sensations rocked through him as his mouth greedily took hers, desire flooding him from all corners and settling in his body part right below his belt.

His hands tightened around her waist when she began to tremble in his arms, and she kissed him back in a way that made everything within him, every single molecule, feel new, revitalized and energized. He couldn't recall the last time he had feasted on a woman's mouth the way he was feasting on hers.

He didn't want to take the time to pause to pull air into his lungs. He just wanted to keep kissing her, continue pressing against her middle to let her feel the hard, solid evidence of just what she was doing to him, how she was making him respond.

The kiss went on, seemed unending until the cell phone in his pants pocket sounded. Of all the times to get a damn signal, he thought, and for a moment he refused to release her mouth, needing to ply it over and over again with strokes of his tongue, although each flick inside her mouth was causing his muscles to contract in a way they had never contracted before.

He hoped the phone would stop ringing but when it didn't, he reluctantly pulled his mouth away from hers, after he'd swept his tongue against her already moist lips.

The ringing had ceased by the time he snatched the phone from his pocket and saw the missed call was a text from Ramsey. He checked the message and it said one word. Bane. Dillon gritted his teeth, wondering what the hell his baby brother had gotten into now.

He glanced over at Pam and thought at that moment he really didn't care, since Ramsey's message had interrupted the most passionate kiss of his entire life. Never had a kiss left him with his senses spiraling out of control and his entire body feeling like it had been torched into flames.

He knew Pam had been as affected by the kiss as he

had. She seemed to be trying to pull herself together. They had done more than just grasped the moment, they had taken total control of it in a way that had them both still scraping for breath.

He watched as she slowly moved away from him to return to the window. She gazed out and he couldn't help wondering if she had reneged and now had regrets. He tensed, refusing to let her off his hook that easily. "Come to my hotel room tonight, Pam."

She swirled around and met his gaze but before she could open her mouth to say a single word, he reached out, pulled her back into his arms and took control of her mouth all over again.

The last time, he had kissed her with a need. This time it was with desperation. He refused to let her incriminate herself in any way, and if kissing her was the way to keep it from happening, then so be it. He would stand here and ply her mouth with his kisses forever if that's what he had to do.

A short while later, when he finally released her mouth, she looked somewhat dazed and her lips appeared slightly swollen. He lifted his hand and pushed her hair from her face, tempted beyond reason to sink his mouth onto hers again. Just the thought of doing so made his hand tremble. He hoped she knew this wasn't the end. Just the beginning.

And to make sure of it, he repeated the words he'd said earlier. "Come to my hotel room tonight, Pam."

Again she looked up and met his gaze. Her lashes fluttered just seconds before she replied, "No."

But before his heart could drop to the floor, she added, "Mr. Davis, the owner of the hotel, knows me, so that won't be a good idea. However, my drama school is only a few blocks away on Durand Street. Will you come there?"

He nodded quickly. "What time?"

"Eight," she said almost in a whisper. "I have a class tonight and everyone should be gone by then."

A moment of silence purred between them and then she searched his eyes. "So, will you come?"

A smile touched his lips and he reached out and stroked her cheek with the back of his hand, leaned closer to her and responded in a low, husky voice, "Sweetheart, nothing short of death is going to keep me away from you tonight."

Six

Pam glanced around at the excited faces of her students. Practice had gone perfectly, with all of them knowing their lines. There was no doubt in her mind that nine-year-old Shauna Barnes had an acting career in her future. Everyone was gearing up for the play Dream Makers Drama Academy would be presenting next month, Charles Dickens's classic *A Christmas Carol*.

"Do you need me to stay behind and help you straighten things up?" Cindy Ruffin asked a short while later, after all the students had been dismissed and were rushing out the door. It hadn't rained as Pam had predicted, but a light layer of snow flurries were coming down.

"No, I'm fine," she said smiling.

Cindy had been a godsend. Her husband, Todd, had

been a classmate of Pam's and, like her, Todd had left Gamble for college. He'd played pro football until an injury ended his career. A few years ago, after Hurricane Katrina, Todd had decided to move his family from New Orleans and back to his hometown. Everyone in town was glad for Todd's return and within a year had talked him into running for mayor.

"I think the kids did an awesome job at practice tonight, don't you?" Cindy asked as a bright, cheery smile touched her lips.

"Yes, and I have to thank you and Marsha for it. You're the ones who have been working tirelessly with them while I've been dealing with paperwork," she said.

"Yes, but having you here is such an inspiration to them since it shows how successful you can be with hard work. You graduated from high school and went off to California to pursue your dream of acting. Do you miss it? All the glitz and glamour of Hollywood?"

Pam thought about Cindy's question. A part of her did miss it, but since she hadn't yet become a part of the "Hollywood crowd" there wasn't a lot she'd had to give up. She had gotten parts in a few low-budget movies, and her dates were mostly those planned by her agent for publicity purposes. She'd spent most of her free time studying her lines for auditions.

"No, I really don't miss it," she said honestly. "At least not as much as I thought I would. I have so much going on for me here."

"Yes, I can see that," Cindy said, glancing down at Pam's engagement ring. "You didn't make an official announcement about your engagement, but I gather a wedding is coming soon. Have you set a date yet?"

Pam swallowed deeply as she looked down at her hand. She had put the ring back on after Dillon had left. Whenever she thought about the kiss they had shared, she could feel her eyes glaze over and her cheeks burn. She had never been kissed that way before. Never.

Clearing her throat she said, "No, not yet."

After a few minutes more of conversation, Cindy left, leaving Pam all alone in the spacious residence that now housed the acting school. Several of the bedrooms downstairs had been converted into office space and classrooms, and the walls had been removed from the entire upstairs area to transform it into one vast studio.

The huge basement had been transformed into a mini-movie-set where scenes could be filmed. It was here at Dream Makers that she had starred in her first low-budget movie for the Gamble theater group. She would always appreciate her very humble beginnings here.

She glanced at her watch. It was a little past seven. She would have a chance to be by herself for a while before Dillon arrived, she thought.

Dillon.

She couldn't think about him without remembering the kiss they had shared earlier that day. And every time she did sensations too numerous to count would invade her body, sending a thrill through her. She'd heard of a man pushing a woman's buttons but, in Dillon's case, he not only pushed them, he had leaned right on them and pretty heavily at that. He had pressed them into another zone. She still felt wired up.

He had left her home shortly thereafter, saying he thought it would be best if he did so, fearing if he were to stay he might not be able to control himself. So she had watched him leave, Jay's journal tucked under his arm, while flutters of desire had overtaken her stomach.

Fletcher had called before she'd left home to tell her he had arrived in Montana safely but wouldn't be returning to Gamble at the end of the week as he'd planned. The insurance company was being difficult, so it would be the first of next week before he got back.

He had asked about Dillon, wanting to know if he was still hanging around town, and she had been up-front with him. Pam had informed him that Dillon had been invited back to dinner and had come to the house to finish going through the items in the attic. She could tell from the tone of Fletcher's voice he hadn't been pleased.

She had dropped by Lester Gadling's office before arriving at the academy and asked him to recheck her father's papers to make sure he hadn't missed something the first time. The attorney had seemed agitated by her visit, and had told her that he would do as she requested, but was confident that nothing would change. She had been hoping that somehow he had made a mistake.

After phoning in and checking on her sisters to make sure everything was okay and all their homework was done, she began walking through all the rooms, tidying up as she went along. As it got closer to eight o'clock, she began to feel a nervousness tugging at her insides. And that same outlandish bout of desire that had overtaken her earlier that day was working its way upward from her toes to her midsection.

There was no doubt in her mind that tonight she and Dillon would do more than just kiss. She knew they would be sharing passion of the most intense kind. They would both give, they would both take and she was truly counting on neither of them having any regrets. Now that she'd thought everything through and was comfortable in her decision, she would admit that she needed him tonight. She wanted him. And she intended to have him.

After pulling into the empty parking lot, Dillon switched off the ignition and checked his watch. Noting it wasn't quite eight o'clock, he decided to stay put for a while.

Adjusting the car seat to accommodate his long legs, he stretched them out in front of him as he released a deep sigh. It seemed as if time had done nothing but drag by since he had seen Pam earlier. He'd nearly gone crazy waiting so he had tried reading more of the journal. So far all Jay Novak had written was information about the dairy business and how well he and Raphel worked together. Apparently, Jay hadn't been suspicious of the relationship between Raphel and Portia.

Dillon's thoughts shifted back to Pam. On the drive over from the hotel he had given himself a pep talk. Getting hyped up over a woman wasn't his typical style, but he'd discovered nothing about him was the norm when it came to Pamela Novak. From the moment he had first laid eyes on her, she had touched him in a way no other woman had ever done before, and that included Tammi.

He checked his watch again and as each minute ticked by so did his need to see her, be with her, hold her in his arms once more. He wanted to run his hands all over her and to taste her with his lips and tongue. He shifted in the seat as he felt his body get hard. It was cold outside, but the inside of his car was getting pretty damn hot.

Dillon tried to switch his concentration to something else, anything else, as he waited. His thoughts drifted to the conversation he'd had with Ramsey a few hours ago regarding the text message he'd sent. Ramsey had gotten an angry call from Carl Newsome. It seemed that Bane was hanging around the man's daughter again and making her dad downright unhappy to the point he'd threatened to do bodily harm to the youngest Denver Westmoreland if he didn't leave Crystal Newsome alone.

Dillon shook his head. For as long as he could remember, Crystal Newsome had been an itch his baby brother just had to scratch. If Bane didn't wise up and leave Crystal alone, that scratch might get him into hot water.

Dillon checked his watch again and after releasing a long breath, he opened the car door and got out. He couldn't recall the last time he'd sneaked around to meet a woman under the cover of night, but as he headed toward the entrance to the Dream Maker

Drama Academy, he had a feeling that tonight such a move would be well worth it.

Pam's feet had touched the bottom stair when she heard the knock on the door. Without wasting any time, she moved in that direction. It was exactly eight o'clock.

As she got closer to the glass door, she could see Dillon through it. He was standing there staring at her with an intense look on his face. That look sent ripples through her body and made her shiver, although the temperature was warm inside. She nervously licked her lips as she opened the door and shivered even more when she felt a blast of cold air.

She quickly stepped back when Dillon walked in, and when he closed the door and gave her his dimpled smile, she felt heat bubbling up inside of her. As usual, he looked good. He had changed clothes and was now wearing dark slacks and a blue buttoned-up shirt. In place of his long coat he now had on a black leather bomber jacket.

She felt ridiculously happy to see him and for lack of anything else, she said, "It didn't rain today like I thought it would."

"No, it didn't rain." The warmth of his response matched the look in his eyes. As she stared deeper she saw that his dark depths seemed more hot than warm.

He glanced around and sensing his curiosity, she said, "Come on, let me show you around." She started to reach out and take his hand and then thought better of it. If she were to touch him now, any part of him, she would probably lose the little self-control she still had. For the next five minutes she took him on a tour of the academy and she could tell he was impressed with everything he saw.

"And the woman who used to live here was once a teacher of yours?" he asked, after she had completed her tour of the upstairs and was ready to show him the basement.

"Yes. Louise Shelton used to be my drama coach and was instrumental in my getting a scholarship to attend college in California. She died within a few months of my returning home after my father died. When she died she willed this place to me, with stipulations."

He lifted a brow. "What kind of stipulations?"

"That I could never sell it and that it would always be used for what it was intended, which was to be a drama academy. I don't have to stay here and run the school per se, but I have to make sure it is managed the way I know Louise would have wanted."

He nodded as he kept walking beside her. A part of her was aware they were wasting time when they both knew exactly what they wanted to do and why they had arranged to meet here at eight o'clock. She was willing to draw things out if he was; however, she doubted he had any idea of how being close to him, walking beside him, was messing with her senses and was stretching what little self-control she had to the limit. When they reached the basement stairs he slowed his steps to let her go first, and she could feel the intensity of his gaze on her again.

It took all she had to put each foot in front of her, being careful not to slip, knowing he was so close behind her, watching her every step. When she reached the bottom floor she turned to wait for him to join her.

And to kiss her.

She had a feeling he knew it. He probably had detected that fact by the way she was breathing, or by the way she was now looking up at him as he moved down the stairs toward her. No doubt it wasn't just one, but all of those things. And really, it didn't matter. What mattered was that he was intuitive enough to pick up on what she wanted and needed, and as soon as he joined her on the bottom floor, he placed his hands at her waist and pulled her into his arms. Before she could draw in her next breath, he leaned down and connected his mouth to hers.

Dillon figured he could stand there and sip on her all night.

Then, maybe not.

Plummeting into her mouth, tasting her like this, with such intensity, such greed and hunger, was making his entire body throb. Desire as thick as it could get, was spreading through him at a rate he could barely control.

He shifted his body, needing her to feel how aroused he was, which equated to just how much he wanted her. And just how much he needed her. He knew she was getting a clear picture when she wrapped her arms around his neck and shifted her body, adjusting it to his so that his erection was resting between the juncture of her thighs. And damn, it felt just like it was where it belonged, he thought.

Well, not quite.

Where it really belonged was deep inside of her. Hell, he was a man, a Westmoreland at that. He knew his male brothers and cousins that he'd grown up with, and he had met the male cousins from Atlanta. So there was no doubt in his mind they all had something in common when it came to basic primitive instincts. They all enjoyed making love to women.

He could imagine taking her all over the place. He wanted to make love to Pam in every room and every single position he could think of and then some. He could certainly get creative rather quickly. But first, this way, starting at her mouth, kissing her with a yearning that made him wonder where in hell a damn bed was when you needed one.

As if she sensed his agitation and the reason for it, she pulled her mouth away, took hold of his hand and led him through an area that looked like a soap-opera film set. They walked through a living room and dining room, caught a glimpse of a kitchen before going around a movable wall that led to a bedroom, one that was decorated with billowy white curtains at a fake window.

On a shuddering sigh she stopped by the bed, and Dillon gazed deep into her eyes. He could tell that she was about to get all nervous on him and decided to say the same words he'd spoken earlier that day. Words she seemed to understand and accept. "You give. I take. No regrets."

She stared at him for a moment and then he watched

as her mouth curved into an easy smile. They would go through with their plans for tonight. No questions asked, no discussions needed. The main thing on his mind was getting inside of her, feeling her wetness surround him, clench him and milk him, which made him decide there was one subject open for discussion and he would initiate it. Birth control.

"I brought condoms," he said, patting the pocket of his slacks. There was no need to tell her just how many since it might scare her.

"And I'm on the pill." She bit nervously on her bottom lip and then added, "And I am not sleeping with Fletcher. I've never slept with him, in case you're wondering about that for health reasons."

Fletcher.

It was only then that he remembered the other man, which made him glance down at her hand. She had taken the ring off again. He wondered why she and her fiancé had never been intimate. Not that he was complaining.

He truly believed she was not a woman who could be in love with one man and sleep with another. That meant there was something about her engagement to Mallard that wasn't on the up-and-up. Sooner or later he intended to get some answers. But not now.

The only thing he wanted to get right now was some of her.

He suddenly detected that her scent had changed and, like a man acutely honed on the woman he wanted, he breathed her into his nostrils, a potent blend of perfume and body chemistry. It was an aroma that could drive a man wild and would make him want to get inside of her real quick and explode all over the place. But only after making sure she was ready to detonate right along with him.

For a long time after Tammi had left he had kept his guard up around women, and had only dated when he got a physical urge to mate as a way to relax, relieve stress and keep his abundance of male hormones in check. But there was something different about Pam, something he'd picked up on the first moment he'd seen her.

She sparked to life something inside of him and he knew making love with her was about more than just blowing off steam. More than great sex. It was about a connection he had never felt before with a woman. A connection on a plane so high it had his insides throbbing.

On a deep, shuddering breath he reached out and tilted her chin up, needing to plunge into her mouth once more, to intensify the connection he already felt. And when she automatically pressed closer to him, he deepened the kiss and slid his arms around her, holding her in a tight grip, as if he never wanted to let her go.

He gave full concentration to her mouth, just as he had done earlier that day. He'd once heard a woman say that you hadn't been kissed unless you'd been kissed by a Westmoreland. Dillon wanted to make sure after tonight that Pam thought the same thing.

So with thorough precision and a masterful meticulousness, Dillon took his time and put his tongue to work. He penetrated it into areas of her mouth that had her groaning, and then he flicked it around in a way that seemed to jar her senses—if the sounds she was making were any indication. He enjoyed kissing her, but moments later he knew he wanted more. Pulling his mouth from hers he took a step back to remove his jacket.

After tossing it across a chair he whispered, "Undress me and then I will undress you." He intended to save her—the best—for last.

A pair of uncertain eyes stared up at him in a way that had him asking, "You have done this before, right?"

He watched a lump appear in her throat as she swallowed, and then she said in a strained voice, "Which part?"

Which part? He lifted a curious brow before responding. "Any of it."

She shrugged her feminine shoulders. "I've had sex before, if that's what you're asking. While in college. Twice. But it wasn't good. Both times it was over before it got started. And I've never undressed a man."

She then lowered her gaze for a second before returning her eyes to his with a flush on her face. "I've said too much, haven't I?" she asked softly. "Given too much information?"

As far as Dillon was concerned, it definitely hadn't been too much information. What she'd just said was something he needed to know. Now he was aware of just what she needed and how she needed it. If any woman deserved to be made love to the Westmorelands' way, it was her. And he intended to do the honors. Proudly. Gladly. Tonight would be a night she wouldn't easily forget. In fact, he planned on taking things slow and making sure every aspect of the evening stayed in her memory forever.

"No, you've told me what I needed to know," he said. In fact, he was sure there had to be more, like why the man she intended to marry hadn't done his job. But they would talk about Fletcher later.

"I'm going to make undressing me worth your while," he said, smiling at her, already imagining her hands on him, all over him. "Go ahead, baby, and do your thing."

She gave him a hesitant smile before reaching out, and the moment her fingers began working on the buttons of his shirt his stomach knotted, and it was all he could do to remember he was supposed to go at a slow pace and not be tempted to speed up the process. This first round would be hers and he intended to make it special for her, even if it killed him.

Pam pushed the shirt off Dillon's shoulders and marveled at how broad they were. She couldn't resist the temptation to touch them, amazed at the strength she felt in them. Then her hands slid to the dark hairs of his chest and she glanced down and saw his hard, flat abdomen. Dillon had a beautifully powerful body, she thought.

Deciding she wanted to check out other areas of that body, she trailed her fingers downward. The moment she did so, she heard his sharp intake of breath and glanced up to his face. The eyes watching her beneath lowered lashes were dark, smoky, sensuous.

Knowing they didn't have all night, she unhooked his belt and pulled it through the loops before tossing it to join his jacket and shirt on the chair. She glanced back up at him. "I need to take your boots and socks off before going any further," she said softly.

He smiled before sitting down on the bed so she could remove his boots and socks. When that was finished, she stepped back as he stood again. Instinctively, her hands went to his waist and she eased down his zipper. Tugging it down wasn't as easy as she'd thought it would be, mainly because of the size of his erection. It was hard to believe that he wanted her *that* much.

"Need help?"

She glanced up at him. "I'll be okay once I get this zipper past here."

He chuckled. "Here where?"

She couldn't help chuckling with him before replying, "You know where. And why do you have to be so big?" Too late. She couldn't believe she'd actually asked that.

Embarrassed to the core, she peered back up at him and saw the huge smile on his face. "This isn't funny, Dillon Westmoreland."

"No, sweetheart, that is the most precious thing anyone has ever said to me."

She knew he was teasing, of course, and after working with his zipper a few moments more it finally cooperated. She was able to tug his pants down his legs as he stepped out of them. Satisfied, she took a step back. There was only one piece left, his briefs. She frowned, wondering why she hadn't thought to remove them with his pants.

"It's not all that serious," he said in a deep, husky voice.

"Maybe not for you, but it is for me," she said, giving him a playful pout. "This is my first time and I have to get it right."

A smile curved his lips. "No, you don't. You can get it all wrong and I will still make love to you tonight."

His words, as well as the determined look in his eyes, did something to her, made her eager to remove his final piece of clothing. She was curious to unveil that part of him that had given her the most trouble. From the way the briefs fit him she had a pretty good idea of just how well-endowed he was. The rest of him was exceedingly toned, definitely virile and oh-so-male.

She inserted her fingers into the waistband of his briefs and gently tugged them down his hips, having no easier time getting them off than she had his slacks. But what removing them fully exposed to her eyes had been well worth the trouble. The man's body was perfect in clothes, but she was particularly enjoying this view of him out of clothes. She had seen a naked man before, but not one this well put together. Not one this large and hard.

"Is there a problem?"

She glanced up and met his gaze, suddenly feeling shy, awkward and unsure of her capabilities where he was concerned. "I hope not," she said softly.

"There *is* not," he countered. "Go ahead, feel your way. Touch it." And then in a lower voice he said, "Get to know it."

Get to know it? She had never fondled a man before in her life but, doing what he suggested, she reached out and first ran her fingers over the tip, fascinated by the feel of the smooth head. Then she traced with her fingertips a path along the sides, marveling at the swollen veins. And when she finally got the nerve to close her hand around him, he moaned out loud.

She quickly loosened her hand. "Sorry, I didn't mean to hurt you."

"It didn't hurt. In fact, just the opposite. Your touch feels good."

She smiled at that. "Really?"

"Yeah."

"Umm, in that case…" She began stroking her hand up and down the length of his thick erection. Her gaze held tight to his face and watched how his eyes became glazed and his lips seemed to tremble. She smiled, satisfied with her efforts and what they were doing to him.

"Not so bad for an amateur, wouldn't you say?" She beamed, feeling like she had accomplished something monumental and proud of herself for doing so. She allowed her hands to get more brazen while watching his erection get harder, and feeling it thicken in her hands.

"I have no complaints," he said in what sounded like a tortured moan. His physical reaction fascinated her, brought out a level of womanly pride that drove her boldness.

"When you're through having your fun then it's my turn," he said in a voice that to her ears sounded like an intoxicated slur.

She considered the wisdom of continuing what she was doing for too long and stole a peek at him from under her lashes. His eyes were closed and his head was tilted back at an angle that showed the veins in his neck. They looked like they were straining. Almost ready to pop.

"Hey, I'm merely doing what I was told. You said to get to know it," she said defensively, but couldn't hide her smile.

Deciding she'd gotten to know him very well, she released him and stepped back and watched as he slowly regained control. Then he stared at her and muttered in a low, throaty voice, "Now it's my time to get you naked."

Getting her naked would be just the start, Dillon thought, looking at her and imagining just how she would look without her jeans and sweater. Even now she looked sexy, with her raven-black hair spilling around her shoulders, a few loose tendrils cascading around her face. Making love to her had been on his mind since leaving her house, and now that he was here, standing stark naked in front of her, knowing that soon, very soon, he would be inside of her sent his entire body into an intense throb mode.

"Come here, Pam," he murmured in a breathless tone, and watched as she didn't hesitate to cover the short distance between them.

When she was within close range, he reached out and snagged her by the waist and brought her closer to the fit of him, and was sure, without a doubt, that she could feel his hardness and his heat, through her jeans.

But he wanted more. He wanted to give her more. Wanted to let her feel more. And with that thought firmly planted in his mind, he reached out and pulled her sweater over her head. Moments later he slung it onto the chair. Her lacy black bra was sexy, but also needed to come off, and he proceeded to remove it. Like her sweater, he sent it flying to the chair.

"Good aim," she leaned closer to say, her breath warm against his throat.

"Thanks," he uttered raspily, his gaze giving her breasts full attention. Her breasts were full, firm twin mounds supported by delicate, feminine shoulders. As if a magnet was drawing his gaze, his eyes were pulled to the nipples and, unable to resist temptation, he took the pad of his finger to flick across both hardened tips.

But he wanted to do more than just look and touch. He wanted to taste them and, with that thought in mind, he leaned in and lowered his mouth to close over a quivering, delicious-looking peak.

"Dillon."

The moment she said his name he stuck out his tongue to run it across a nipple before pulling it into his mouth to suck in all earnestness. He didn't even try to change his stance when she lifted her hand to support the back of his head to keep right where he was, to continue what he was doing. Not that he intended to stop. The taste of her breasts was arousing him and, with an easy movement, he shifted his mouth to the other nipple to greedily ply it with the same attention.

By the time he lifted his head and met her gaze he could barely keep his entire body from trembling. A need for her, to make love to her, surged through him and he stooped down on bended knees to remove her shoes and socks. To maintain her balance she placed a hand on his shoulder and her touch sent his muscles rippling as sensations roared through him, made him clench his teeth.

After removing her shoes and socks, he stood, straightened his body to his full height and without saying a single word he reached for the waistband of her jeans. Somehow he managed to hold it together until she stood before him in nothing more than sexy, black, lacy, high-cut panties. They were panties he would be taking off her and he was fighting the urge to just rip them off her instead.

Getting back on his knees he began lowering her panties down her long, gorgeous legs, and sucked in a deep breath when her scent surrounded him. He shot a glance upward and saw the heated look of desire in her eyes.

It took all his strength to stand, and without wasting any more time, he reached out and swept her into his arms. Holding her gently he moved to the bed and together they tumbled back onto the covers.

Seven

Pam felt her stomach stir when she gazed up into Dillon's eyes. She had ended up on her back between his firm thighs, with him towering over her. At that very moment she felt several things. Captured. Ensnarled. His.

She forced the last from her mind immediately. How could a woman be engaged to one man and possessed by another? She didn't want to be confused by anything now, and she certainly didn't want to think about Fletcher. This was her time, this sensual interlude, her moment to seize something she might never have again.

You give. I take. No regrets.

And from the eyes bearing down on her and the arms locked on both sides of her, she had a feeling Dillon

Westmoreland was more than ready to take everything she had to give. And there would be no time for regrets.

He began lowering his head and she lifted hers upward to meet his mouth. The moment they touched, he began devouring her with a hunger and need that she felt all the way to her toes. He had kissed her greedily before, but this was a different kind of ravenousness, one that bordered on insatiability. As if, no matter how many times he kissed her or how deep and thorough the kisses, he would never be able to get enough. However, that didn't mean he wouldn't try. And in this case, trying meant using his tongue to pleasure her in a way she'd never been pleasured before. No man before had taken so much time, had concentrated on so much detail during a kiss. It was a practice that he'd perfected and she was the satisfied recipient.

He gave all and held back nothing. Provoking her, tempting her, almost demanding of her to give back. So she did, by boldly returning his kiss with his same voraciousness. She wrapped her arms around his neck as he sank his mouth even deeper onto hers. Her response was wanton, her desires keen and her senses at the moment were shot to hell.

He broke off the kiss at the same time his hands began to move all over her as he held her gaze. Starting at the center of her throat, he slowly inched a path downward toward her chest. When he reached her breasts and ran the pad of his thumb across the protruding tips, pleasure, as sharp as it could get, rammed through her and she almost forgot to breathe. And when he leaned closer to replace his fingers with his mouth, she felt heat circulate then settle between her legs.

When he brought his tongue into the mix she gasped. Suddenly she felt full as if she needed to scream out, but could not. The most she could do was summon up enough energy to moan. Then his mouth released her breasts and he began trailing a heated path down to her navel with his tongue. He seemed fascinated with her belly button and she felt his wet tongue all around it. She shuddered as her stomach tightened and then relaxed, over and over again.

And when she thought he would be returning to her mouth, he shifted his body, lifted her hips and dipped his head. The moment the scalding tip of his tongue went inside her womanly core, she emitted a loud moan. At the same time, she heard his growl of male satisfaction. It was evident from the way he was using his tongue inside of her, that he enjoyed this type of lovemaking. He went about it with such ardent dedication that she was nearly in tears. She was pinned between his mouth and the mattress. She realized that he didn't intend on letting her go anywhere until he got his fill.

And he didn't intend to be rushed.

He was meticulous in his lovemaking, pushing her just to the peak, driving her close to the edge again and again. She couldn't suppress her response and groaned shamelessly, holding firm to his shoulders while she was his enjoyment. And even moments later when she let out a scream as a tide of pleasure came crashing down on her, his mouth remained locked on her, as if determined to savor every last bit of her.

It was only later, when she felt weak as water and was panting for breath, that he lifted his mouth to withdraw from her. He leaned back on his haunches, licked his lips and gave her a smile that made her come all over again.

There was nothing more beautiful than seeing a woman clutched in the throes of ecstasy, Dillon thought, as he studied Pam's features. And just knowing he'd been the cause sent desire clamoring all through him and made his already hard body feel harder.

With her glazed eyes on him, he eased off the bed to reach for his pants. Going through the pockets he pulled out several condom packets and tossed all but one on the nightstand. He then proceeded to put the one on, knowing Pam watched his every move.

He was a man who'd never had a problem with his nakedness and the thought that he was on display, exposed and being checked out from head to toe, didn't bother him in the least. The only thing on his mind was making love to the woman in that bed. And what a picture she made. Sexy. Naked. Exposed. It seemed that she didn't have a problem with nudity, either, and he was glad of that.

He returned to the bed and drew her to him, needing to hold her, needing to touch her, needing to kiss her. His mouth found hers again and he moved his hand downward toward her parted thighs. Inserting a finger inside of her, he captured her gasp right in their kiss.

He even swallowed her moan when his finger began moving inside of her, slowly with determined and well-defined strokes, glorying in her wetness, breathing in her aroused scent. All the while their mouths and tongues were mating greedily, and with a need that he felt in every part of his body, especially his throbbing shaft.

Not sure he could last much longer, he pulled away slightly to ease her back deep into the mattress as he shifted into position, simultaneously spreading her thighs and locking her hands above her head in his.

He changed positions again to get the lower part of his body in perfect formation, with the head of his erection right at her entrance. And then, while she watched him, he began lowering his body, surging inside of her. The moment his head came in contact with her heat he wanted to thrust inside, but felt that this was something he had to savor, even if it killed him.

And with every inch he pushed inside of her, he felt as if he was literally dying. She was tight and her body muscles clamped down on him, clutched him for all it was worth, and in response he released her hands to grip her hips, determined to go as deep inside as he could go.

A world of absolute pleasure began closing in on him, engulfing him with an urge to move. He cupped her bottom closer, so he could delve deeper, and with slow, steady strokes, he began staking his claim on her. Every time he slid inside of her and every time he slid out, he felt a sharp pull on his sanity, an increased dose of pleasure and a fortitude to drive into her the same heated, silken force that was driving him.

It worked. She began moving with him, joined him, clenched him, milked him to the point he felt everything was getting pulled out of him. He locked his legs with hers and then, while buried deep inside of her, he began flexing his lower body in a way to get as close as he could get, sinking into her deep, mating with her hard, thrusting into her rapidly. And when she screamed his name, he threw his head back when the same infused pleasure that ripped through her, tore through him.

And the name that he moaned from his lips was hers. The body he was exploding inside of was hers. And the lips he knew he had to taste at that very moment were hers.

Everything was about her, as well as her ability to make him feel things no other woman could make him feel was artfully and enticingly being transmitted in a satisfying way. Emotions he couldn't define, and not just on a physical plane, energized his muscles and made his hunger for her that much more intense. Making love with her wasn't just good, it was brutally good. So good he actually felt whipped. His senses shattered in a thousand pieces and, as sensations continued to race through her and spread into him, he felt a sense of fulfillment he knew that he could only find with her.

Pam wondered if she would have the ability to ever move again, and wasn't sure if she even wanted to. Even now she was wrapped in Dillon's arms, their legs entangled, their arms entwined and their bodies still intimately connected. She felt drained, worn out, deliciously sated in a way that almost made her purr.

The way he was draped across her, she didn't have to move her head to look into his eyes, since he was there, staring at her with the same amazement and sexual fulfillment in his eyes that she felt in her body. This was what Iris had wanted her to experience at least once in her life and now she was glad that she had. This had been the ultimate in sexual satisfaction, the most gratifying, mind-blowing passion.

She had used muscles she hadn't ever used before, and she'd found every part of him, both working and nonworking, to have a definite purpose. She could only lie in awe, while her heart tried to slow down from beating so fast in her chest.

She felt cherished, protected and desired. Not only in the way he was looking at her, but at the gentle caress of his hand moving on her thigh, like he still had to touch her in some way, even in the aftermath of shared sexual bliss.

Pam moved her lips to say something but no words came out. It was just as well, because he leaned up and captured her mouth in his. She raised her hand to his cheek, needing to touch him, and to feel the movement of his mouth on hers beneath her palm.

When he finally broke the kiss she felt perfectly contented and when he finally released her, slowly pulled out of her to go to the bathroom, she felt a profound sense of loss. She watched for him to return and when he appeared, lounging naked in the doorway, his long, muscular legs braced apart, she thought his stance had a masculine sexiness that almost made her drool. Her gaze moved all over his body and the main thing she couldn't help but notice was that he was fully aroused again.

Seeing him in that state did something to her own body—made her feel alive, wanton, desired. His gaze scorched her, as he slowly scanned her entire body, lingering on her legs before moving upward to the juncture of her thighs. And there his gaze stayed, transfixed for a spell, and she felt the heat of it on her womanly core. She forced down a deep, shuddering breath when he began moving toward her and she couldn't help noticing the swell of muscles in his broad shoulders and the wide expanse of a strong, solid chest.

He paused by the bed, giving her a totally male smile while he proceeded to put on another condom. She watched the entire process, unable to force her gaze away. A heavy silence hung over the room.

And then she sat up in the bed and opened her arms to him. He moved, placed a knee on the bed, went into her arms and planted his mouth on hers. And as he adjusted their positions to ease her back deep onto the bed, the thought that continued to run through her mind was that tonight was their one and only time together. She desperately wished it could last.

A few hours later, they stood fully dressed together in the foyer of the academy. It was a little past midnight and time for them to part. Together they had stripped the bed and changed the linen. Then she had made them a cup of hot chocolate and they'd sat down at the kitchen table. Not much was said between them, as there was nothing left to be said. They were both deep in their own thoughts.

He had Jay Novak's journal back at the hotel, so he

couldn't use the excuse of visiting her place to read it. But he wanted to see her again. Be with her again. In fact, he intended to be a part of her life.

He mentally scrambled to make sense of that decision and released a deep breath when he finally did. She had touched a part of him in a way he could not walk away from. She might have assumed this was a one-night stand, but as far as he was concerned that was not the case.

He didn't harbor any guilt that he was no better than Raphel in cutting in on another man's territory. If nothing else he had discovered, before even kissing her that first time, that she really didn't belong to Fletcher; at least not the way a woman should belong to the man she was about to marry—heart, body and soul. Totally and completely.

Now was still not a good time to bring up that fact and ask why she would even consider marrying a man she didn't love, a man who hadn't introduced her to passion. At first he'd thought he could get beyond that curiosity, deciding it was strictly her business. But that was no longer the case. Now it was his business, as well, mainly because as far as he was concerned Fletcher Mallard was not the man she needed.

He was.

Some may consider him thinking such a thing as arrogant, possibly even a little egotistical, and they probably would be right in their assumption, he thought. But something had happened tonight in that bed, something he couldn't dismiss. Every time he went inside of her, he'd felt more than just sexual pleasure. He'd felt a sense of belonging. He'd felt a connection he could not explain and a deep, abiding need to claim her.

As far as he was concerned he wasn't taking anything away from Mallard, because it was quite obvious that the man didn't have a claim on her anyway. The only stamp Mallard had on her was the ring she had placed back on her finger. And, although he didn't particularly like the sight of it there, he would tolerate it for now.

His gaze moved from her hand to her face. She was staring out into the night. It was time to leave but neither was making an effort to do so. He knew he couldn't mention to her what he was thinking. For whatever reason she had decided to marry Mallard. He had news for her, but it wouldn't be delivered tonight. He would give her time to make her own decision about things—namely in his favor. And if she didn't, then he would intervene. He was the one who had introduced her to passion and he would be the one who would continue on with her lessons.

In the meantime, he would learn what kind of hold Mallard had on her to make her agree to a loveless and passionless marriage.

At that moment she looked up and met his gaze and he knew, whether she realized it or not, she was now his. That conclusion sent an immediate jolt to his nervous system, stimulated his brain and made every muscle in his body feel a strength of resolve he hadn't felt in a long time. He needed time to think, but for now, he'd just accept things the way they were.

Silently, he reached out and began buttoning up her

coat. Surprised, she blinked, then smiled up at him while studying his face. "Thank you. You take such good care of me."

He smiled back, deciding not to tell her the reason he did so was because she belonged to him. Instead, he said, "You've been too hot to suddenly have to get cold."

She laughed and then reached out and placed her arms around his neck. "Yes, I have been hot tonight and all because of you. You're special, Dillon. I've known you for only a short time, but it seems like I've known you my entire life."

He understood what she was saying, because he felt the same way about her. He'd never been a man who would lay claim to a woman after sleeping with her just one time. But with Pam, things were different. He didn't know how, he just accepted that they were.

He felt his lips curve into a smile as he asked, "I never believed in that paranormal stuff, but do you think we could have been together in another life?"

He watched her brow furrow and then moments later the answer was in her eyes. "No," she said. "Nothing would have obliterated from my mind the kind of passion I felt tonight had I shared it once before with you," she said and smiled.

"What I shared with you tonight is something I've never shared before with any man. So there has to be another reason why I feel so free and uncontrolled with you."

He felt the same way. There had to be a reason why he felt free and uncontrolled around her as well. But whereas she might accept what they had shared tonight as a casual affair, he could not. If she figured he would just walk away, leave Gamble and head back to Denver without a second glance, then she was wrong. Dead wrong.

And to show her how wrong she was, he raised a hand to her face and caressed her cheek. "Tonight was very special to me, Pam. I've never met a woman quite like you."

He could tell by the look in her eyes that she didn't know what to make of his words. That was fine because soon enough she would. He lowered his head and captured her lips in a slow yet greedy fashion. He felt her shudder beneath his mouth and when she tightened her arms around his neck, he deepened the kiss.

He wanted her. And he would have her. As far as he was concerned, she was already his. That was the Westmorelands' way. The ability to recognize his or her true mate when he encountered her or him, although they might initially try to deny it. He would be the first to admit some Westmorelands were stubborn, and he had discovered that trait wasn't confined to just the Denver clan. He'd been told that the Atlanta Westmorelands were just as bad.

He could now admit that he had made a mistake with Tammi in thinking she was the one. He felt certain there was no mistake with Pam. And for him to be so sure of that so soon might be a mystery to some, but not to him.

He slowly and reluctantly withdrew from her mouth, but for the moment he refused to release her from his arms. "I'm walking you out to the car and then I'm following you home to make sure you get there safely," he whispered against her ear.

She pulled back and a cautious look appeared on her face. "You don't have to do that."

"Yes, I do." For *reasons you can't possibly imagine,* he thought. But he simply asked, "Ready to go?"

"Yes, but…" She studied his face. "Tonight…"

She didn't continue, but nervously moistened her top lip with her tongue, an action that had him forcing back a rush of desire.

"What about tonight?"

"Tonight was tonight. Tomorrow remains the same. I'm engaged to Fletcher."

He looked down at her. A shaft of light from the fixtures in the parking lot came through the glass door and slanted across her face, making her look so beautiful he felt his heartbeat increase. He silenced the response he really wanted to make—one that clearly stated her engagement was evidently in name only and regardless, she was his, signed, sealed and so deliciously delivered. His stomach clenched just thinking about their lovemaking.

Her expression indicated she expected him to understand and to accept her words. There was no use telling her he wasn't about to do either. Instead, he knew he would do what he had to do. The first thing was to find out why she had gotten engaged to a man like Mallard in the first place.

So to bide his time, he pushed a strand of hair back from her face. "I know," he said.

Those two words were all he was capable of saying to her right now. "Let me walk you to the car."

She held back, refusing to move an inch as she studied his face for a moment. "You don't need to come to the house tomorrow, do you?"

He swallowed deeply. She was trying to cut ties now. She didn't have any regrets about tonight but she knew she couldn't continue. "No, I'll take the next couple of days and stay at the hotel and relax and read the journal. If you need me for anything, you know where to reach me."

She nodded and then moved toward the door. He walked by her side. He would give her two days and if she didn't come to him, engaged or not engaged, he would be going after her.

Eight

"We don't understand, Pammie. Why did Dillon stop coming for dinner?"

Pam glanced across the dinner table at Nadia, knowing how her baby sister operated. Nadia would ply her with the same question until she got what she considered a satisfactory answer. Pam wasn't sure that her response would be satisfactory, but judging by the three pairs of eyes staring at her, Nadia wasn't the only one waiting to hear what she had to say.

Pam could make it easy on herself and place the blame on the three of them by claiming they were the ones who'd scared him off, and that Dillon had been fully aware of their little matchmaking schemes at dinner and preferred to have no part of it. But telling her sisters that would not be the truth. Dillon had said on more than one occasion that he enjoyed her sisters' company and that they reminded him of his female cousins back in Denver. He had taken their shenanigans in stride and hadn't seemed bothered in the least.

"Pammie?"

Nadia's soft voice pulled her back to the moment and she glanced across the table. Before Pam could open her mouth to answer, Paige spoke up in a disheartened tone. "He doesn't like us any more than Fletcher does, does he?"

Pam was taken aback by her sister's assumption. "That's not true. Dillon really likes the three of you and enjoys dining with us, but he has our great-grandfather's journal and has been doing a lot of reading over the past couple of days. You must not forget the reason he came to town in the first place."

She took in a deep breath before continuing. "And as for Fletcher, you girls are wrong about him. He does like you."

"Then why is he planning to send us away after the two of you get married?" Nadia asked with a belligerent look on her face.

Pam was surprised by her sister's question. "Where on earth did you get such an utterly absurd idea? Fletcher is not planning to send you away after we get married."

Nadia's frown deepened and a worried look lit her eyes. "He is, too. He told Gwyneth Robards's father that he is, and her father told her mother, and Gwyneth overheard them talking and she told me."

Pam frowned. Gwyneth Robards was Nadia's best friend. Her father, Warren Robards, owned a slew of sporting goods stores across the state. He and Fletcher were good friends. Pam was not one to believe in gossip. She wished Nadia wouldn't do so, either. "Nadia, there's no way Fletcher would have said something like that."

"So, are you saying Gwyneth's father lied?"

Pam frowned. "What I'm saying is that Gwyneth apparently misunderstood what she heard from her parents' conversation. Again, there's no way Fletcher could have said that."

What she didn't add was that he knew why she was marrying him—to save her family home, to secure a future for her sisters and to keep the family together. Even if they were to lose their home, her sisters would return to California with her or they all would remain in Gamble and make do.

"Getting back to Dillon, Pam," Jill said. "I don't care how much reading he has to do, he has to stop and eat sometime. Did you invite him to dinner the last three nights?"

Pam nervously bit down on her bottom lip. She hadn't invited Dillon to dinner the first night because they had planned their secret meeting that night at the academy. And she hadn't invited him the past two nights because she had needed time to get herself together after their night of passion.

"No," she finally said. "Like I said, Dillon has a lot to read. He said as much the last time he was here."

"So you will invite him back?"

Pam's stomach knotted. Again, three pairs of eyes focused on her. "Yes, I'd invite him back but it's up to him whether he would come. Like I said, there's a reason why he came to Gamble and it's not to keep us entertained."

As if satisfied with her answer, her sisters resumed eating their dinner and the conversations then revolved around what had happened at school that day. She was glad their interests had shifted to other things, although hers remained on Dillon. Every time she thought about that night and all the things they'd done and shared, she would get all flushed inside, her body aching for a repeat. There was no doubt in her mind that if she were to see Dillon now, her body would weaken. If he were to make an attempt to kiss her, or even remotely suggest he wanted to take her to bed again, she would not be able to resist him.

She hadn't talked to him or seen him since that night. He had left a message for her on the answering machine yesterday indicating he'd decided to change hotels and had checked into one in Rosebud. Unlike Gamble, the neighboring city of Rosebud had a number of cell towers in close proximity so there was always a signal. She understood that he would want to stay connected to the outside world since he was a businessman.

He had provided the name of the hotel, which was only a ten-mile drive from Gamble. She had thought about calling him back to let him know she'd gotten the message, but had eventually talked herself out of it. She knew she would see him again, because eventually he had to return the journal. She was hoping that by then she wouldn't be thinking so much about how his kisses had felt on her lips, or just how good he'd felt going into her body. And then, how she'd felt when he was inside of her. She tightened her thighs together at the memory.

She licked her lips and then picked up her glass to take a sip of her cold tea, needing to relieve her suddenly hot throat. She forced her thoughts to shift to what Gwyneth thought she'd overheard about Fletcher's plan to send her sisters away. She'd ask Fletcher about the rumor when he called later that evening. She figured that he would be calling before she left for her evening class at the academy.

Halfway through dinner the phone rang and she pushed her chair from the table and crossed the room to answer it. "Yes?"

"How are things going, Pamela?"

A part of her wished she could feel some excitement, some fluttering of sensations anywhere in her body at the sound of Fletcher's voice, but that wasn't happening. Her heart slammed painfully in her chest at that realization. "Everything is fine, Fletcher. How are things with you? Is that problem in Bozeman getting corrected?"

"Yes, in fact, I have good news. I might be back in Gamble this weekend instead of next Tuesday."

She swallowed deeply and tried to put a smile in her voice. "That is good news."

"And do you know what would make me extremely happy, Pamela?"

She dared not try to guess. "No, what?"

"If you've decided on our wedding date by the time I return. I know you prefer waiting until February, but I want to marry this year, so a Christmas wedding is what I prefer."

All of a sudden she felt her stomach drop. Christmas was next month. "I can't possibly get things together by then."

"What do you need to do other than show up at the church? Besides, I hate to bring this up, but I'd like to satisfy that mortgage on your home as soon as possible. That's one of my wedding gifts to you."

Pam's eyes narrowed. In his own passive-aggressive way, Fletcher was reminding her of the reason she had agreed to marry him. "I'm sure you want that matter resolved and done with as soon as possible, right?" he added.

"Yes, of course."

"So will you have a date for me when I get back to Gamble?" he asked.

She stole a glance at the dining room table where her sisters were chatting away. They had happy looks on their faces and she was determined to keep it that way. They were smart, all three of them, and she'd made a promise to herself at her father's funeral to do whatever it would take to make sure they got the best life had to offer.

"Pamela?"

She breathed in deeply. "Yes. I'll have a date for you but I won't promise it will be this year."

He didn't say anything for a moment and then she

heard the frustration in his tone. "Let's start with the date and I hope it's one we will both agree to."

Knowing he was probably about to ask her about Dillon, she quickly jumped in to say, "Nadia is bothered about something, Fletcher, and I'm sure it's all a mis-understanding, but I thought I'd mention it anyway."

"What?"

"She thinks you're sending her away when we get married. I assured her that wasn't the case and—"

"That has crossed my mind."

Pamela stopped talking in midsentence. Her hand tightened on the phone. "Excuse me?"

He must have heard the cutting anger in her tone. "Calm down, Pamela. It's not what you think. You have smart sisters and I think they're getting a wasted education going to that public school in Gamble. As you know, I went to a private school and I received a top-notch education. The best. And I know you want Nadia and Paige to get accepted into a good college. Going to a private high school will not only assure them a good education, but also entrance into the best colleges. That's what you want, right?"

"Yes, but—"

"And just think, they would be associating with people who will benefit them in the long run."

"Yes, but I'm not for sending them away from home," she whispered, so her voice would not carry to the dining room. She had just assured Nadia that she wouldn't.

"I know, which is why I'm looking into schools in Cheyenne. That's not too far away," he said, as if she would be glad to hear the news.

She moved away from the kitchen and into the living room, which would afford her more privacy. "As far as I'm concerned, if it's not here in Gamble then it's too far away."

"But we'll be looking out for their futures. There's a wonderful private school there that has excellent living facilities and great security."

Pam tried to keep a ripple of anger from consuming her. "You should have talked to me about this first, Fletcher."

"It was going to be another one of my wedding gifts. I know how much your sisters' futures mean to you."

Pam closed her eyes. "We can discuss this more when you return."

"I don't understand why you're upset. I'd think it would be what you wanted. At least I believe it's what you told me you wanted that day you accepted my marriage proposal."

Pam couldn't say anything. Was it really fair to get upset with him when she *had* said those things?

"If that's not what you want, Pamela, then no sweat. I want to do whatever makes you happy," he said in a throaty, low voice that did nothing but frustrate her even more.

"I know, Fletcher, and I appreciate everything you're doing, but we'll need to talk about this when you get back."

"Okay, baby. Have a good evening. And by the way, is Dillon Westmoreland still in town?"

She could actually hear the coldness in his voice. "No, in fact Dillon has left town," she said. What she'd just said really wasn't a lie because Dillon was no longer in Gamble. Fletcher didn't have to know he had merely moved to a hotel in neighboring Rosebud.

"I guess he got what he came for and decided to move on. That's good. Maybe we won't be seeing the likes of him again anytime soon," Fletcher said cockily.

She frowned, not liking Fletcher's attitude. "I suspect he will be returning at some point since he still has my great-grandfather's journal." She figured she might as well prepare him now so he wouldn't go into cardiac arrest when he did see Dillon again.

"He can keep the damn journal for all I care. I just don't like the man."

Pam inwardly fumed. The journal was not his to decide whether Dillon could keep it or not. "Goodbye, Fletcher."

"Goodbye, Pamela, and I hope to see you Sunday."

Dillon smiled at all the voices he heard in the background of his phone conversation with his brother Micah. Micah, a graduate of Harvard Medical School who was only a couple of years younger than Dillon, was an epidemiologist with the federal government. Everyone often joked about Micah being the mad scientist in the family.

"So how long will you be home, or did you just drop in long enough to attend this weekend's charity ball?" Dillon asked Micah. His brother was known to travel all over the world doing work for the government. He had lived in China for an entire year during the bird-flu epidemic.

The charity ball he was referring to was the one the

Westmoreland family hosted every year to raise money for the Westmoreland Foundation they had established to aid various community causes.

"I'm here for the ball and I'll be home at least through New Year's. Then I'm off to Australia for a few months."

"Good to hear. I plan on flying in for the ball this weekend," Dillon said. A part of him really wasn't ready to put distance between him and Pam, even for a short while.

"I heard Sheriff Harper talked you into taking his sister Belinda as your date," Micah said in a teasing tone.

Dillon rolled his eyes. "It was either that or have Bane spend a night in jail for trespassing on the Newsomes' property in the middle of the night." He wasn't sure he appreciated his brother finding his predicament with Belinda so amusing. His brothers and cousins knew Belinda had had her eye on him as husband number three for about a year.

"So how is the investigation into Raphel's past coming along?"

"I'm finding out more and more information about our great-grandfather every day," Dillon replied.

Micah chuckled. "Just as long as it's nothing that can come back to haunt me with the State Department. I can barely handle the fact that he ran off with those other men's wives."

Dillon smiled. "I told you the real deal about Raphel and Lila. He did it to protect her."

"Yes, but we still don't know what was up with him and the second one, Portia Novak. It should be a rather lively discussion at Thanksgiving dinner this year and will be the first time in a long time everyone will be home."

After a few more minutes of conversation with Micah, the phone was passed around to the rest of his brothers and cousins. Everyone wanted to know what information about their great-grandfather he'd been able to uncover so far. He didn't tell them everything he'd found out, but he felt he'd told them enough for now.

It was close to six in the evening when he finally said goodbye to everyone and hung up the phone. He glanced over at the journal he'd been reading over the past two days. He was surprised no one in the Novak family had taken the time to ever read the journal. If they had they would have learned just why Raphel had taken Portia away, and why Jay had given him his blessings to do so.

He glanced around the hotel room. It was totally different from the one he'd had in Gamble. It was a lot more spacious and the furnishings were early American instead of Victorian. Although CNN was alive and well on the big-screen television and the reception for his cell phone was perfect, he would be the first to admit that he missed the huge bathtub at the Gamble hotel. But he needed to be in a hotel that had fax and Internet service. His firm was working on a huge multimillion-dollar deal and he needed to be available if a last-minute snag developed.

And he needed to be someplace where if Pam wanted to pay him a visit, it wouldn't make the six o'clock news.

He walked over to the window and looked out. It was cold outside but nothing like it had been the night he'd met Pam at her drama school. He sucked in a deep breath when he remembered that night and how it had changed his life. He hoped she'd gotten his message about changing hotels. The one in Gamble was closer to her place, but this one was only ten miles away.

She hadn't returned his call so a lot of things were going through his mind right now. Had she broken their rule about not having any regrets? Had Fletcher made it back to town? He didn't have answers to those questions, but the one thing he did know for sure was that if he didn't hear from her tonight, he would be making a trip into Gamble to see her. He still had her journal and tomorrow would be a good time to return it.

On the drive from Dream Makers back home later that night, Pam was trying, really trying, not to recall her conversation with Fletcher earlier that day. She was even trying, as hard as she could, to give him some slack and believe he had her sisters' best interest at heart when he'd made the decision they should continue their education in Cheyenne and not in Gamble. But for him not to have discussed it with her was totally unacceptable.

He of all people knew how close she and her sisters were. Did he honestly think she would let them go off and live at some private school, leaving their family and friends behind? And as far as she was concerned, there was nothing wrong with public schools. She'd gone to one and had done pretty damn well.

She reached out to turn up the dial for the heat a little. It was cold, although it wasn't as cold as it had been the last night she'd driven home from the academy. That was the night she had spent almost three hours in Dillon's arms. She couldn't help but smile just thinking about it.

She had talked to Iris but hadn't told her best friend a single thing. She hadn't needed to. According to Iris, there was something in the tone of her voice. She sounded relaxed. It sounded like she'd taken a chill pill. Pam chuckled as she remembered the conversation.

She passed a road sign that indicated the exit to Rosebud was coming up. She immediately felt a pull in the lower part of her body and it wasn't a gentle pull. It was a voracious tug. She tried to keep staring through her windshield, determined to keep her eyes on the road and to drive straight home. She then began experiencing flutters in her belly and her nipples pressing against her shirt felt sensitive.

The physical reactions her body was going through just knowing she was an exit away from Rosebud made her release a quiet moan. The hotel where Dillon was now staying was less than five miles from the interstate.

Dillon had given her his hotel room number when he'd left the message, but had made it seem as if he'd provided the number for informational purposes only. As if he'd wanted to assure her the journal was still safe and in good hands. Now she couldn't help wondering if perhaps he'd had an ulterior motive. Was he hoping to see her again, although she'd made it clear that what they'd shared that night was a one-night stand?

But the biggest question of all was why she was contemplating getting off at the next exit. And she knew the answer without thinking really hard about it. She was thinking of doing so because she needed to see him.

She needed to be with him.

She sighed deeply and as she took the exit to Rosebud she refused to question her sanity any longer. She was merely enjoying an indulgence that would be denied to her forever once she married Fletcher.

Dillon lay in his hotel room in the dark. He had dozed off, after eating a meal that room service had delivered and taking a bath. The television was on but he wasn't watching it. Instead his thoughts were on the woman he wanted.

He wondered what she was doing. Did she think about their night together as often as he did, or had she put it out of her mind? He had just shifted positions in the bed when he heard a knock at the door. Assuming it was housekeeping coming to turn down the bedcovers and to make sure he didn't need anything else before they retired for the night, he slid out of bed and into the jeans he'd placed on the back of the chair.

He opened the door slightly, just enough to make out his visitor and, when he did, sensations tore into him and forced air through his lungs. He quickly opened the door wide.

He refused to ask Pam what she was doing there. For a second he seriously doubted he had the ability to utter a single sound, so they stood there for a long moment and stared at each other, speechless. He did glance down at her finger. She had taken the ring off again. He looked back up into her eyes and felt his pulse rate increase.

Then she broke through the silence and smiled. "Are you going to invite me in?"

"Baby, I plan to do a whole lot more than that," he muttered thickly, his gaze not leaving hers.

He took a step back and she entered his hotel room. He closed the door behind her.

"I guess you're wondering why I'm here," she said in a quiet tone.

He shook his head. "We'll talk about the *why*'s later. Right now I just want to hold you. Make love to you. I've missed you."

"And I've missed you, too," she said honestly, wondering how she could miss him so much after two days, when she hadn't missed Fletcher at all and he'd been gone nearly twice that long.

Knowing they didn't have a lot of time on their side tonight, she took in his solidly muscular, naked chest and the way his jeans rode low on his hips. They were unsnapped and the zipper was barely up, which meant he had slid into them rather quickly. She hoped he was ready to slide out of them just as fast.

Feeling her heartbeat almost out of control, she shifted her gaze from him to glance around the room. Her great-grandfather's journal sat in the middle of a wingback chair.

She returned her gaze to him, knowing he'd been watching her intently and was probably waiting for her to make a move. She decided to do so. Moving away from the door she crossed the room to him and, the minute she stood in front of him, his arms easily slid around her.

"I hope I'm not interrupting anything," she said, reaching up and placing her arms around his neck.

He gave her a dimpled smile that was so sexy she felt her knees weaken. "Nothing at all. In fact I was just thinking about you."

"You were?"

"Yes."

And if to prove that point, he pulled her closer against him and she felt the erection he wasn't trying to hide. The magnitude of it resting snugly against the juncture of her thighs felt hard and hot. "And just what were you thinking about?"

"This." And then he swept her into his arms and kissed a startled gasp from her lips.

He took her mouth with a greed that made her moan in his arms as he placed her on the huge bed. And he continued to kiss her as she felt the heat of his body over hers. Whenever he kissed her like this, he had the ability to make her forget everything but him and how he was making her feel. Her thighs were nested between his and, although they were fully dressed, she could feel every hard and solid inch of him.

Slowly he withdrew from her lips, and as she stared deep into his eyes she caught the light from the lamp that brightened the eyes looking at her. And she knew at that moment that she could see a mirror of herself in his eyes. What she saw was a woman fiercely attracted to the man she was with and thinking she didn't want to be anywhere else.

"I want to show you how much I've missed you," he said huskily, kneeling before her while running a fingertip along the side of her face.

She met the intensity of his gaze, recalled every single thing he had done to her the previous time and felt her inner muscles clench at the thought he would be doing so again. That in itself made her lean up and whisper the challenge. "Then show me."

"With pleasure," he whispered close to her lips before taking those lips to begin a slow, sensuous mating that she felt as a gentle throb between her thighs. This kiss had all the high intensity, provoked the stirring sensations of the kisses they'd shared that night, but she could feel something different this time. It was there in the way he wielded his tongue in her mouth. He kissed her with a possessiveness that made every cell in her body become hypersensitive. And by the time he freed her mouth from his, she could only stare up at him, totally and fully at a loss for anything except the man gazing back at her. The look in his eyes clearly said he was claiming her. Here and now.

Warning bells sounded in her head. She knew what the outcome of her future had to be. He did not. She had to marry Fletcher—she didn't have a choice in the matter. It was something he would not understand and something she could not let him or anyone else prevent. It didn't matter what sacrifices she knew she was making. What mattered most to her were her sisters.

She hoped the vibes she was beginning to intercept from him were wrong and that he was not considering anything beyond what they had shared this week. Maybe she'd made a mistake in coming here tonight. Had removing her engagement ring made him think that she was willing to put aside her future with Fletcher? She had to make sure he understood that was not the case.

"Dillon?"

He reached out and placed a finger to her lips and, as if he comprehended what was going through her mind, said softly in a husky tone, "Although I don't have all the facts, I do understand, sweetheart, more than you know, and I think it's time for you to understand something, as well. Regardless of who you might be engaged to marry, you *are* mine."

Before she could comprehend his words, he lowered his mouth to hers in a kiss that was as potent and powerful as any intoxicating drug. And it was just as effective. Her mind and body became meshed in a mirage of sensations so forceful she gave up any desire to convince him to think differently.

She only recalled bits and pieces of him removing her clothes. But she did vividly remember the kisses he placed all over her naked body once he had completed the task. And she had committed to memory the sight of him removing all of his clothes, every single stitch, and then putting on a condom—almost a difficult task due to the size of his arousal—before returning to her.

Concentrated desire consumed her the moment he rose above her as he took her mouth again the way a hunter would go after his prey. Moments later he pulled away to use that same mouth to trace downward, to latch on to her nipples, sucking gently and causing flutters to stir within, to the point of being breathless.

And then he was there, close to her face, raising her hips, widening her thighs, lifting her legs to hug his shoulders, and then entering her in one smooth thrust that made her moan his name. But he didn't stop there. He continued to stroke her, inside and out, bearing down on her mind each time like he was bearing down on her body. And with each stroke it seemed to relay words he had not yet spoken, words she felt each time his dark eyes met hers, each time they breathed in and out together as one.

Sudden tears sprung to her eyes when she realized the depth, the intensity and then also the uselessness of the love she felt for him, all the way in her bones, in the air she was breathing. Yes, she had fallen in love with him. She'd once heard that a woman's body could and would recognize its mate, and the thought that this man was hers almost overwhelmed her, and touched her very soul.

He saw the tears flow down her cheek and leaned in to kiss them away, as if he had the ability to make whatever was wrong in her life right. She wished it was that simple, but knew it was not.

She looped her arms around his neck when his mouth moved from her cheeks to her mouth, and then she kissed him in all the ways she had dreamed of kissing him the past two nights.

He gave in, allowing her to lead, to take the kiss wherever she wanted it to go and to whatever degree of passion she wanted it to be. And when she felt the explosion that ripped through her body to ricochet to his, she couldn't hold back her scream of pleasure. And when she felt him sink deeper into her, tail-spinning into his own massive release, she clutched him tighter to her, locked her legs around his back, knowing that, regardless of what he thought and no matter that she now knew she loved him, this was all they would have together.

Nine

"I want to know why you are marrying a man you don't love," Dillon said raspily, close to her ear.

They lay locked in each other's arms, their bodies entwined, drenched in sweat from the intensity of their lovemaking. The aftermath of pleasure was so profound they were still fighting to get their heart rates back to normal while they savored what had to have been passion of the most explosive kind.

Dillon watched as her gaze widened at such a deliberate and bold question, and then his heart began pounding in his throat while he waited for her to respond. When she nervously licked her lips, he was tempted to lick right along with her but knew he had to hold back and listen to what she had to say. Tonight he wanted answers and wouldn't be satisfied until he got them.

And then, not surprisingly, fire crept into her eyes and she tilted her chin slightly. "You have no right to ask me that," she said.

A smile touched his lips. His woman was feisty when she needed to be and he liked that. He liked even more the thought of her as *his* woman. "I have every right, Pam. I'm a Westmoreland, remember. Raphel's great-grandson. I take what I think is mine regardless of whom it might belong to at the time. And you are mine. I told you that. And if you have any doubt of that take a look at the position you're in. I'm still inside you because it's where I want to be, where I know you want me to be."

She frowned. "Doesn't my engagement ring mean anything?"

He was tempted to laugh at that question. "No, not even when you're wearing it. And I notice that you don't hesitate to take it off when it suits you to do so," he said, knowing his words would stir her fiery anger even more.

At the moment he didn't care. He had fallen in love with her. If he hadn't been sure of it before, he'd known it as fact the moment she had taken the initiative and had plied him with her kiss. It seemed while she'd been ravishing his mouth with her tongue, emotions he had never felt before, deeper than he'd ever thought they could go, had consumed him, broken him down and reeled in his heart.

"Remember what I said? I give, you take and no regrets? I may have forgotten to mention that in rare situations, I claim. This is one of those situations."

She shifted to ease up but he had her leg pinned beneath his. Her frown deepened and then she said, "It's complicated, so it won't do any good to tell you anything."

"Humor me. Tell me anyway."

She looked away from him but he heard her words nevertheless. "What makes you think there is something to tell?" she asked.

"Because you're here in this bed with me, and by your own confession a few nights ago, you've admitted you've never slept with Mallard, the man you're engaged to marry. And," he said, reaching out and tilting her chin upward, bringing her face back in focus to his so their gazes could meet, "you're not a woman who could be in love with one man and sleep with another."

"You don't know that," she all but snapped.

He continued to hold her gaze as he took her hand, led it to his lips and then placed a kiss on her knuckles. "Yes, I do."

For some reason deep down she actually felt that he did. No, she wasn't a woman who could love one man and sleep with another. In all actuality, he was the man she loved, but it would take more than love to help her now.

"Pam?"

She breathed in deeply and said, "I *have* to marry Fletcher."

He lifted a bemused brow. "Why?"

She hesitated for a moment before saying, "My father died and left a second mortgage on our home. Although I've worked out a monthly payment arrangement for now, which is being handled through my father's attorney, the bank in Laramie wants the loan paid in full within ninety days. I tried applying for a loan with a bank here in town but that didn't work out. Fletcher had offered to marry me to take care of it. And he's promised to make sure money is there when my sisters need it for college."

Dillon just stared at her. At first he wasn't sure he'd heard her correctly. Then to make sure he had, he asked in an incredulous tone, "You're entering into a marriage of convenience?"

She nervously licked her bottom lip. "No, not quite. He does want children one day, so it will not be a marriage in name only."

"If Mallard wants to impress you with kindness why didn't he just pay off the balance of the loan for you?" he asked, biting out the words through clenched teeth.

She looked surprised he would suggest such a thing. "I couldn't ask him to do that. I'm talking about a balance that's over a million dollars. Dad purchased adjoining land with the intention of reopening the dairy."

"Even if Mallard couldn't loan you the money, he could have cosigned for you to get it," he said, not accepting any excuses for the man. He could recall the number of times his signature had been on such a document for his family members. "And most banks require that loans of that amount be insured in case the borrower dies," he added. "Which bank holds the mortgage?"

"Gloversville Bank of Laramie. I guess somehow Dad got around it, which I still find rather strange. But

I've checked with his attorney and he's gone over Dad's papers more than once. Dad didn't have the kind of insurance that would satisfy the loan. Mr. Gadling has been most helpful, working with the bank on my behalf, setting up the monthly payment arrangements where he receives the money from me to pay them."

Dillon heard what she was saying but it didn't make sense. In his profession he didn't know of any bank that would loan that much money without requiring that some kind of life insurance be purchased with it.

"So there," Pam pronounced.

She'd said it like that settled it, but he had news for her. It didn't. His gaze traced over her features. A part of him saw beyond what she was saying. It saw beyond what she thought she needed. She assumed she needed Fletcher Mallard. As far as he was concerned, she needed him. And unlike Mallard, he would deliver without any strings attached. It could only be then, after the matter with Mallard was dispensed with, that he would ask her to marry him, for all the right reasons two people should marry.

But still, something about the way her father's loan had been handled bothered him and he intended to check a few things out for himself on Monday. Deciding it would be best not to tell her what he planned to do, he lowered his head and tasted her lips instead, stirring the embers between lovers back to a roaring blaze.

And moments later, when he eased back inside her body, he knew he was where he belonged.

* * *

"Where do you get so much energy?" Pam asked in a whisper, while watching Dillon ease from the bed and head toward the bathroom. He glanced over his shoulder and smiled at her. "You, Pamela Novak, give me strength."

He moved on toward his destination giving her a good view of strong, long legs and a nice, tight tush. He gave her strength, as well, she thought, closing her eyes and snuggling under the covers. She inhaled the masculine scent he'd left behind and knew at that moment, as crazy as it seemed, and unlikely as it could be, each time they made love she fell deeper and deeper in love with him.

Now he knew the whole story regarding her relationship with Fletcher, and although she had a feeling he didn't like it, at least she hoped he understood why she *had* to marry Fletcher. Shifting up in bed she glanced at the journal on the chair, just as she heard Dillon returning from the bathroom.

"Did you find out any more about why your great-grandfather ran off with my great-grandfather's wife?" she asked, trying to keep her focus on her question and not on his naked body.

"Yes, I found out," he said, walking over to the chair to pick up the journal and returning to the bed to hand it to her. "I marked the spot with a sticky note. Some members of your family had to have known the whole story, but I guess it was a family secret."

Pam lifted a brow before opening the journal to begin reading. A few minutes later she was lifting astonished eyes to his. "Portia was caught in bed? With another woman?"

Dillon nodded slowly. "Yes. And to protect her from the scandal it would have caused, the husband of the other woman and your great-grandfather decided it would be best to keep the matter between them. But it was decided both men would eventually divorce their wives, which during that time would have been a scandal in itself."

Pam nodded. "So since Raphel was about to leave Gamble anyway to head out to California, he and Jay came up with this plan to take Portia away so she could start a new life elsewhere. Do you think the other woman joined her later?"

Dillon shrugged. "Who knows? We're talking about the nineteen thirties. There's no telling how things turned out with Portia. But your great-grandfather did legally divorce her for desertion before marrying your great-grandmother. I'm glad to finally know why Raphel ran off with another man's wife for the second time."

Pam closed the journal. With the mystery solved, Dillon would be leaving Gamble. He had no reason to stay. "Both times Raphel came to the rescue of women who needed his help. Sounds like a high-caliber man, a real protector of women," she said.

His lips curved into a smile. "Yes, but so was Jay. He could have made things hard on Portia, but he was willing to step back and give her a chance to live her life the way she wanted to live it. Leaving with Raphel was still a scandal within itself, but it would have been far worse had the truth been revealed."

He took the book out of her hands and placed it on the nightstand before easing back into the bed with her. "I'm flying out in the morning to return home to take care of a few family matters, but will return by the end of the week," he said.

Confusion touched her face. "But why are you returning? You've gotten what you came for. You now know the reason Raphel ran off with Portia. He and Jay set the entire thing up to look that way to protect Portia's reputation."

"Yes," he said huskily, easing up on his knees in front of her and slowly advancing on her like a hunter stalking its prey. "That was the reason I came initially, but you're the reason I'll be coming back."

"B-but nothing has changed. I still need to marry Fletcher."

A dimpled smile touched his lips. "No, you don't. I'm a man known to make things happen instead of taking advantage of a situation like I think Mallard is doing, so I plan to offer you an alternative."

She lifted a brow. "An alternative?"

"Yes. I can't let you marry another man when I know that I'm the man for you."

She shook her head and gave a resigned sigh. She'd thought he understood, but he really hadn't understood at all. "Dillon, please listen to me, I—"

"No, I'm asking you to trust me," he said, gazing into her eyes with a plea that she felt all the way to the lower part of her belly. "I know that is a lot to ask when we've only known each other for a short period of time, but I believe there has to be another way out of this situation. A way in which you don't feel forced or obligated to marry Mallard or anyone else. I want you to trust me and give me time to find another way. Do for me what Jay did for Raphel. Trust me to make your situation better."

She stared deep into his eyes and then she said softly, "Fletcher expects me to have a date set for our wedding when he returns."

Dillon nodded. "When does he get back?"

"Sometime this weekend, probably Sunday."

"Then stall him. I need time to check out a few things," he said huskily. "Say you will trust me."

She continued to look into his eyes, searched his face for a sign of why she shouldn't trust him and knew she would not see one. "I will trust you."

A satisfied smile touched his lips. Raising his hands, he cupped the lower part of her face and leaned forward for their mouths, as well as their bodies, to mate once more.

Ten

"Pamela, I thought we agreed that you'd set a date for our wedding by the time I got back," Fletcher said, sitting down to the dinner table with her and her sisters.

He had called Sunday morning to say he would be arriving back in Gamble around noon and was eager to see her. She had invited him to dinner and the first thing he'd done, after giving her a hug and telling her how much he had missed her, had been to ask what day she had picked for their wedding.

"Maybe she's decided not to marry you after all, Fletch," Jill said, smiling sweetly over at him with a deliberate glare in her eyes.

"That's enough, Jillian," Pam said to her sister. Jill

didn't know how true her words were. "I've been busy, Fletcher."

He frowned. "Too busy to plan a wedding that we both know needs to take place?"

She frowned back, wishing he wouldn't discuss such matters in front of her sisters. "We can talk about this later, Fletcher." She knew he didn't like putting off the discussion. In truth, she didn't, either.

Thanks to her sisters dinner hadn't been pleasant. They had practically ignored Fletcher. Having been gone for almost a week, he had wanted to be the center of attention and hadn't liked being ignored. Although she had tried rallying conversation around him, Nadia, Paige and Jill had not bought into her ploy. He hadn't been any better, often times mocking things they'd said. By the end of dinner her nerves were strained and she was ready for her sisters to retire to bed and for Fletcher to leave.

"Oh, I almost forgot," Fletcher said, breaking into her thoughts as she walked him to the door.

"My private plane made a pit stop at the Denver airport and I went inside to grab a copy of a magazine and noticed today's *Denver Post*. Your friend made the front cover with a very beautiful woman plastered by his side when they attended a charity function together this weekend. According to the paper, wedding bells might be in order for the couple," he said, smiling brightly. "I figured you'd want to see a copy so I saved the article for you."

She lifted a brow, confused. "What are you talking about?"

"This." He pulled the folded article from an inside pocket of his jacket and handed it to her.

She unfolded the article that had been neatly clipped from a newspaper, and it took all she had to hold back a gasp from her lips. Before her eyes was the man she had fallen in love with, dressed handsomely in a tux with a very beautiful woman by his side. The two were smiling for the camera. Although there wasn't an article associated with the photo the caption read, "Is Romance Brewing for These Two?"

She swallowed and glanced back up at Fletcher who was watching her intently. "You seemed bothered by that photograph, Pamela. Is there a reason why?"

She lifted her chin and met his gaze. "You're wrong," she lied. "I am not bothered by it." In truth she was. She and Dillon had just spent time together a few nights ago. He had said he had to return to Denver. Now she knew why.

Fletcher smiled. "Now I think it's time I put my foot down regarding our wedding plans," he said, reaching out and catching her by the waist and pulling her closer to him. His move surprised her because he had never been so forward with her before. Being close to him did nothing for her or to her. It didn't have the same effect on her that Dillon had. Because she loved Dillon, and the thought that she meant nothing to him, that his words had all been lies, was too much.

"Put your foot down how?" she somehow managed to ask.

"I've been trying to be patient but more than anything

I want you as my wife, Pamela. I'm aware you're not in love with me, but I believe over time that you will come to love me. I offered you marriage to help you out of a bad situation, but evidently you don't see it as such anymore. And maybe the thought of losing your home and securing your sisters' futures aren't the big deal they once were."

"That's not true."

"Then prove it. I no longer want a wedding date. Now I want an actual wedding. This week. A very private affair. Here on Friday. Make it happen or come Saturday our engagement is off."

Her eyes narrowed. "Are you forcing me into marriage?"

His smile widened. "No, sweetheart, it's your choice. Good night, Pamela." He then opened the door and left.

Pam stood in the same spot and stared down at the photograph in her hand. She angled her head to study the picture. Dillon was smiling. The woman was smiling. Had they been merely smiling for the camera or for each other, she wondered.

And come to think of it, the issue of whether or not there was a special woman in Dillon's life had never come up. She had never asked and he'd never offered any information. All she knew was that he was divorced, nothing more.

But he had asked her to trust him while he checked out a few things. Came up with an alternative.

She closed her eyes for a moment and leaned against the closed door. Had she read more than she should have into that request? Deciding the only person who could answer that question was Dillon himself, she crossed the room to use the phone, but then realized she didn't have his phone number. He'd never given her his number. Had there been a reason for him not doing so?

She glanced down at her watch. It wasn't quite nine o'clock and Roy Davis at the River's Edge Hotel would probably have information about Dillon on file. She would have to think of a good reason why she would need him to give it to her.

She released a long sigh when Mr. Davis picked up the phone. "The River's Edge Hotel."

"Mr. Davis, this is Pamela Novak. How are you?"

"I'm doing fine, Pamela, how about you?"

"I'm fine, but I was wondering if you could help me."

"Sure thing. What do you need?"

"Dillon Westmoreland's home number. I know he stayed at the hotel for a few days last week and I need to reach him. He left something here when he visited," she said.

"Hold on. Let me check my records."

It didn't take Mr. Davis but a few moments and he was back on the phone reading off a phone number to her.

"Thanks, Mr. Davis."

"You're welcome, Pamela."

As soon as she disconnected the call she quickly dialed Dillon's number. The phone was picked up on the third ring. "Hello?"

Pam's breath caught in her throat and her hands trembled as she hung up the phone. A woman had answered.

* * *

"So now, when are you going home?" Dillon asked the woman who was sprawled on the floor in front of his television set watching a movie.

He had come out of the shower a few moments before to find her there. Ramsey had warned him that he would regret the day he'd given Megan a key to his house. His twenty-six-year-old cousin Megan was an anesthesiologist at one of the local hospitals. She was okay to have around until she got underfoot. Like now.

"And why aren't you at your house watching your own television?" He walked through his living room on his way to the kitchen.

"It's a scary movie and I don't like watching these types alone."

He rolled his eyes. "Did I hear the phone ring a few moments ago?"

"Yes, a wrong number I think," she said, not taking her eyes off the television. "Do you mind if I crash here tonight?"

"Nope. I'll probably be gone when you wake up anyway," he said, opening the refrigerator.

That got her attention and she turned away from the television and glanced across the breakfast bar at him. "But you just got back."

"And I'm gone again. This time to Laramie. I have business to take care of there."

Dillon took a drink of orange juice right out the carton while thinking about his business in Laramie. He couldn't help but think about Pam. He missed her like hell. He had been tempted to call her but because Fletcher was probably back he had decided against it. He didn't want to make waves just yet. He hoped she trusted him enough so she could tell Mallard that she wasn't going to marry him at all. Dillon had promised to give her an alternative. An option in which she wouldn't feel compelled to marry for anything less than love. In a way he wished he'd never left Gamble or, better yet, had asked her to come home with him and be his date at the ball. But he had promised the sheriff that he would escort his sister. He'd felt obligated to keep his promise. He had pretended he had been having a good time, but had been missing Pam the entire time, which hadn't been fair to Belinda.

Then he'd really gotten ticked off to find his picture plastered on the front page of this morning's paper with a caption suggesting there was something between them. The last thing he needed was for Belinda to get any ideas, especially since he was in love with Pam. That's why he was determined to be able to offer an alternative solution to Mallard's marriage proposal, so that he could go to work to capture her heart the same way she had captured his.

Pam woke up early the next morning and, before she could talk herself out of doing so, she dialed Dillon's number again. Just like the night before, a woman answered. This time in a sleepy voice.

And again Pam quickly hung up the phone.

She felt a tug at her heart and knew she could not

depend on Dillon to come through with an alternative
solution any longer. He was back home and back into
the arms of a woman who undoubtedly meant something to him. She had to remember that he had not
promised her anything. *He gave. She took. No regrets.*
But that still didn't stop every bone in her body from
aching with the strain of heartbreak.

At least she had gotten a taste of passion that was so
rich and delicious, she would savor it in her memories
for years to come and they would be there to help her
through the years ahead.

She drew in a deep breath. Her decision was made.
She picked up the phone to make another call. This one
to Fletcher. His voice, also sleepy, greeted her on the
second ring. "Hello."

"Fletcher, this is Pamela. I'll make sure everything's
set for our wedding on Friday evening."

Dillon had caught a plane early Monday morning to
Laramie and went straight to Gloversville Bank from
the airport. There he met with the bank president.

"Mr. Westmoreland, I recognized your name immediately," the man said, smiling from ear to ear. "Are you
looking to do business in Gloversville?" he asked,
offering Dillon a chair the moment he'd walked into the
man's office.

Dillon was glad he had recognized Roland Byers as
someone he'd once done business with a few years ago
when the man had worked at a bank in Denver. "No, but
I would like some information on one of your customers."

Byers raised a brow as he took the seat behind his desk. "Who?"

"Sam Novak. He passed last year and I'm helping his daughter close out his affairs. We were wondering why his loan wasn't paid off when he died. The balance was over a million dollars."

Confusion touched the man's face. "Umm, I don't see how that's possible. We require life insurance on all loans for that amount. Hold on a moment while I check. I can't give you any specifics of the loan due to privacy laws, but I can tell you whether it's still active."

Dillon watched as Byers called his secretary on the intercom and provided her with the information needed to look up the file. In less than five minutes the woman walked into the office carrying a folder, which she handed to Byers.

It took Byers less than a minute to glance through the papers, look over at Dillon and say, "There must be some mistake because our records are showing the loan is paid in full. That information, along with the appropriate papers, were given to Mr. Novak's attorney, Lester Gadling, almost a year ago."

"I can't believe you're actually going to go ahead and marry the guy," Iris said in a disappointed voice. "What about Dillon?"

Just hearing his name nearly brought tears to Pam's eyes. "There's nothing about Dillon. It was a fling, nothing more."

"But I thought he said he would—"

"I don't want to talk about it, Iris. Now, can you make it here by Friday?"

"Of course I can make it, although I prefer not to. But if you're determined to make a huge mistake, the least I can do is to be there and watch you make it."

The moment Dillon walked out of the bank and was seated in his rental car, his cell phone went off. He answered it immediately. "Hello?"

"Bane's in trouble. We need you home."

Dillon drew in a deep breath, released it as he shook his head and snapped in his seat belt. "Okay, Ramsey. What has Bane done now?"

"Eloped."

"What the hell!" Dillon nearly exploded. "And please, whatever you do, don't tell me it's with Crystal Newsome."

"Okay, I won't. But I will tell you that Carl Newsome is going to make sure he goes to jail this time for sure."

Nothing like a death threat to get the Westmorelands together under one roof for something other than to eat or to party. Dillon glanced across the room and stared at his baby brother and wondered if Bane would ever outgrow his bad-boy mentality. You couldn't help but love him even when you wanted to smash his head in for not having a lick of sense.

Luckily, they had found him before Carl had, although it had taken nearly two full days to do so, and had included traveling to five different states. It had been obvious that he and Crystal hadn't wanted to be found. It had also been quite obvious they'd been having so much fun that they hadn't taken the time to swing by Vegas for a quick wedding after all.

That had made Carl Newsome somewhat happier. He hadn't needed to put out the expense for a quick divorce. Something had happened years before to make the Newsomes and Westmorelands modern-day Hatfields and McCoys. Something about a dispute over land ownership. As a result, Newsome would never allow his daughter to marry a Westmoreland.

Now they were all at the police station where Bane had been charged with kidnapping, although Carl knew good and well that Crystal had gone willingly. Crystal had even said as much. She'd even gone so far as to admit to being the one who had planned the entire thing. She thought she was in love with Bane, but at seventeen her parents thought she didn't know the meaning of love. Bane thought he was in love with Crystal, as well.

"The judge has made a decision," Sheriff Harper said as he came back into the conference room and got everyone's attention. "Carl Newsome is willing to drop the charges as long as Bane agrees never to see Crystal again."

Bane, who had been leaning against the wall, straightened and angrily yelled, "I won't agree to a damn thing!"

Dillon rolled his eyes, shook his head and asked the sheriff, "And what if he doesn't agree?"

"Then I will have to lock him up and, since he violated the last restraining order with the judge wherein he promised not to set foot on Carl's property, we will transfer him to the farm for a year."

Dillon nodded as he looked across the room at his baby brother, held Bane's gaze a moment and then said to the sheriff, "He *will* agree."

"Dil!"

"No, Bane, now listen to me," Dillon said in a firm voice that got everyone's attention in the room. He had lost time in returning to Gamble and he wasn't too happy about it, especially now that he knew the attorney for Pam's father had lied to her.

"Crystal is young. You are young. Both of you need to grow up. Carl mentioned he plans to send Crystal away to live with an aunt anyway. Use that time to finish college, get a job at Blue Ridge. Then in three to four years she will be old enough and mature enough to make her own decisions. Hopefully, by then the two of you will have college out of the way and can then decide what you want to do."

He saw the misery in his brother's features. "But I love her, Dil."

Dillon felt Bane's pain because he knew, thanks to Pamela Novak, the intensity of love. "I know you do, Bane. We all know you do. Hell, even the sheriff knows, which is why we've overlooked a lot of you and Crystal's shenanigans over the years."

It didn't take a rocket scientist to know that Crystal and Bane were sexually active. Hell, Dillon didn't want to recall the number of times he'd come home from work unexpectedly to find the two had cut school, or how he would get a call in the middle of the night from the sheriff after finding Bane and Crystal parked somewhere when neither Dillon nor Carl had been aware they were out of their houses.

"But it's time for you to finally grow up and accept responsibility for your actions. Go to college, make something of yourself and then be ready to reclaim your girl."

Bane didn't say anything for a moment as he switched his gaze from Dillon to stare down at the floor. Everyone in the room was quiet. And then he looked back at the sheriff. "Can I see her first?"

Sheriff Harper shook his head sadly. "Afraid not. Carl and Crystal and her mother left a short while ago. It's my understanding they are taking her to the airport to put her on the next plane to an aunt living somewhere in the South."

Bane, with shoulders slouched in defeat, didn't say anything for the longest time and then he turned and walked out of the room.

Ramsey leaned against the door with a cup of hot coffee in his hand and watched Dillon pack. "You're leaving again?"

Dillon nodded as he continued to throw items into his suitcase. "Yes, I should have been in Gamble long before now, and I haven't been able to reach Pamela to explain my delay."

That had bothered him. He had tried more than once to phone her but either she was out or was not taking his calls and he couldn't understand why. He couldn't wait to meet with her father's attorney to find out just why he had lied to Pam, making her think that there was still an outstanding loan balance in her name. For some reason Dillon couldn't dismiss, he had a feeling Mallard was behind Pam's fictitious financial problems.

"Well, good luck. I hope your flight leaves on time. A snowstorm is headed this way."

"I heard," Dillon said, zipping up his suitcase. "That's why I'm heading out now. I'm hoping my plane can take off before it hits."

Ramsey took a sip of coffee. "I take it you're serious about Pam Novak."

Dillon smiled as he grabbed his coat off the rack. "Yes, and I intend to marry her."

Dillon did get stuck at the Denver airport due to the snowstorm, and it was noon the next day before he arrived in Gamble. He was upset that he still hadn't been able to reach Pam. He hadn't spoken to her since last Friday and here it was Friday again.

Once he arrived in Gamble he went straight to Lester Gadling's office, deciding to let the man explain things before going to see Pam to let her know what he'd learned. He got to Gadling's office only to discover he was out to lunch, so Dillon waited.

It was close to three o'clock before Gadling returned and, when the secretary told him Dillon had been waiting for him, he looked at him nervously before asking if he had an appointment.

"No, I don't, but I need to talk to you about Sam Novak."

"What about Sam Novak?"

Dillon didn't like the fact the secretary was sitting there all ears. "I prefer talking to you about this privately," he said.

Gadling seemed to hesitate for a moment, then he asked, "And what relation are you to the Novak family?"

"A friend."

Moments later Dillon followed Gadling into his office and as soon as the door closed behind them, the lawyer asked nervously, "And what is it you want to know?"

Dillon didn't hesitate. "I want to know why you've led Pam to believe she owes a balance on her mortgage. I know she doesn't, so you better have a good answer for me, Mr. Gadling. And I want to know what happened to those payments she's been making to you every month."

"I don't have to tell you anything," the man said.

Dillon gave him the smile that all his family members knew meant business. "No, you don't have to tell me anything. I can always call the state attorney's office to let them know about attorney fraud."

That got Gadling's attention. He went around his desk and to Dillon's surprise pulled out a bottle of scotch, filled a shot glass and gulped the liquid down. "I didn't want to lie. It was Fletcher Mallard's idea. I am being blackmailed."

Dillon stared at the man for a long time and then sat in the chair in front of Gadling's desk. "I think you need to start at the beginning."

The man began talking and Dillon listened. Every so often Dillon's hands would clench into fists at how Mallard had manipulated both Gadling and Pam to get what he wanted. Pam actually thought Fletcher Mallard had come to her rescue, not knowing he had orchestrated the entire situation.

"So, there you have it. Mallard was so obsessed with marrying Pamela Novak he would have done anything to have her at his mercy."

Dillon's jaw twitched. "I'm going over to the Novaks' and bringing Pam back here. I want you to tell her everything that you've told me."

The man seemed surprised at his request. "That might be hard to do."

Dillon leaned forward. He refused to accept any excuse from the man. "And just why might that be hard, Gadling?"

"Because she and Mallard are getting married today. In fact, the wedding is probably taking place as we speak."

Eleven

"Please, Pammie, you don't have to marry him," Paige said with tears in her eyes.

"And why didn't you want to talk to Dillon when he called this week?" Nadia asked. "Why couldn't we pick up the phone when caller ID said it was him?"

Pam closed her eyes and looked across the room at Jill who hadn't said anything but whose eyes were narrowed. She then looked at Iris who looked just as upset. "Listen you guys, this is *my* wedding day."

She then turned her attention to Paige. "And I do have to marry him. You don't understand now but one day you will.

"The reason I didn't want to talk to Dillon this

week is rather complicated, but I had my reasons," she said to Nadia.

She ignored Jill's undignified snort. "Come on, Reverend Atwater just arrived and we need to get this over with."

Pam glanced over at Iris, glad her friend had kept her mouth shut for once. Iris had been giving Pam an earful all morning. "Well, how do I look?" Pam twirled around the middle of the room in the new dress she had bought earlier in the week.

"Too damn good for that asshole," Iris said under her breath; however, Pam's sisters heard the comment. Pam frowned when her sisters fought to hold back their giggles.

"Okay, ladies, let's go," she said to everyone. "The minister is waiting."

Dillon didn't give a damn if he was going over the speed limit as he raced his rented car to the Novaks' place. Gadling's news that a wedding was going on and that Pam was the bride had sent him running to his car and tearing out of town at breakneck speed. It was a wonder the sheriff was not on his tail.

He had tried calling Pam before leaving Gadling's office but evidently someone had taken the damn phone off the hook.

He let out a deep breath when he finally pulled into her driveway and saw three cars parked in front of the house. He recognized the one belonging to Mallard but not the other two.

He had barely switched off the ignition before he

was opening the car door and leaping out. At this point he cared less if he was late and she had already married Mallard. If that was the case then she would become a kidnapped bride, a feat a Westmoreland was gifted in crafting.

The minister's words floated over Pam, but her thoughts were on Paige. That morning, Pam had found her baby sister sitting on the side of the house crying. Paige was unhappy because today Pam would be marrying Fetcher Mallard. And Pam knew her other two sisters felt the same way.

Her father's death had left all three of her sisters in her care and at that very minute Pam realized their happiness meant more to her than anything else. And if marrying Fletcher was causing them this much distress then there was no way she could go through with it.

Reverend Atwater's words then rang out. "If any man can show just cause why these two people shouldn't lawfully wed, let him speak now or forever hold his peace."

She opened her mouth to put an end to the ceremony, knowing she couldn't let it continue, when a male voice boomed from the doorway of her home, loud and clear. "I can show just cause!"

Pam swung around and her heart literally jumped in her chest when she saw Dillon standing there with a fierce frown on his face. He was moving quickly toward her.

"What is he doing here?" Fletcher asked loudly through clenched teeth.

"Looks like he's coming for Pammie," Paige said

smartly with a huge smile on her face, clapping her hands with glee.

Pam could only stare at Dillon, too shocked to move or say anything.

"What the hell do you think you're doing here?" Fletcher said, coming to stand in front of Pam, blocking Dillon's way.

A smile curved Dillon lips when he looked down at Fletcher. "What does it look like? I'm stopping the wedding. So move aside, I need to talk to Pam."

"I'm not moving," Fletcher snapped.

The curve in Dillon's lips widened. "I have no problem in moving you, trust me."

"Gentlemen, please," the minister was saying.

It was then that Pam found her voice. She moved around Fletcher to stand in front of Dillon. She met his gaze. "Dillon, what are you doing here?"

She saw the intense look in his eyes. "I asked you to trust me to come up with an alternative."

Pam's eyes narrowed. "I did until I called Sunday night and *she* answered the phone."

He raised a confused brow. "She who?"

"You tell me."

"Look, Westmoreland, I don't know why you're here but you're interrupting our wedding," Fletcher said in an irritated tone.

Dillon shifted his gaze from Pam to Fletcher and glared at the man. "There *won't* be a wedding." He then glanced back over at Pam and said, "We need to talk privately."

Pam stared at him for a moment and then took a step back. "No, we don't."

"If she doesn't want to talk to you, I do," Iris said. When Dillon glanced over at her, Iris smiled. "I'm Iris, Pam's best friend."

When Pam shot her best friend a glare, Iris shrugged her shoulders. "Hey, what can I say? He's a cutie."

Dillon shifted his gaze back to Pam. "We do need to talk, Pam," he said, crossing his arms over his chest. "If you don't want to talk in private then I can very well say what I want right here. Fletcher and Lester Gadling lied to you. There is no balance owed on this house or land. Your father did have the necessary insurance to pay it off. Fletcher was blackmailing Gadling to claim otherwise. And those monthly payments you made on the loan were going to Mallard."

"That's a lie!" Fletcher said loudly. "How dare you come here spouting lies!"

"It is not a lie. Pam can verify everything I've said with Gadling. You weren't counting on her finding out the truth until after the two of you were already married, and by then you were hoping she would be so beholden to you that it wouldn't matter."

Pam turned to Fletcher, shocked at Dillon's allegations. "Is that true, Fletcher?"

Fletcher reached out and grabbed her hand. "Pamela, sweetheart. Please understand. I did it to give you all the things you deserve. I had to get you to marry me some way."

She angrily shook his hand off her and took a step back.

The expression on her face was one of total rage. "You deliberately lied to me. Just to get me to marry you?"

"Yes, but—"

"Please leave, Fletcher, and don't come back."

He looked at her and then shifted his gaze to Dillon before moving it back to Pam. "Don't hold out for Westmoreland to marry you, if that's what you're thinking about doing," he snarled. "Remember that article I showed you? The one from the *Denver Post*. He already has a woman back in Denver, so I'm the best catch around these parts. When you want to renew our relationship, call me." He then turned and angrily stalked out of the house.

"Pam, we need to talk," Dillon said once the door had closed behind Fletcher.

She glanced up at him and narrowed her gaze. Placing her arms across her own chest, she said, "No."

His lips curved into a dimpled yet predatory smile and Pam had the good sense to step back. But she wasn't quick enough. Dillon reached out and swept her off her feet and into his arms.

"Put me down, Dillon!"

He gazed down into her angry face. "No. You are going to listen to what I have to say."

He then glanced at the minister's shocked expression before smiling at Pam's sisters and Iris. "Excuse us for a moment. We need to discuss something in private."

Ignoring Pam's struggles, he headed toward the kitchen and closed the door behind them.

"Put me down, Dillon!"

"Certainly," he said, sitting down in a chair and keeping her pinned to his lap. He looked down at her. "It seems I need to get a few things straight. First, that picture Fletcher was referring to that was in the *Denver Post* was about a date I had agreed to months ago. The woman, Belinda Harper, is the sheriff's sister. I owed him a favor for all the times he's helped me keep Bane out of jail."

When she didn't say anything, just continued to glare at him, he continued. "And the woman who answered my phone Sunday night was my cousin Megan. She stayed over at my place until Monday. In fact, I left her there to catch my flight into Laramie to check on things at Gloversville Bank."

Now, that got her attention. He watched as she lifted a brow. "She's your cousin?"

"Yes, I told you I have three female younger cousins. Megan, Gemma and Bailey."

He paused and added, "I would have gotten back to Gamble sooner, but we had trouble with Bane again, which I had to return to Denver to take care of. And then there was that blasted snowstorm that hit Denver. I got stuck at the airport."

Pam held his gaze. "You were trying to get back?" she asked as if still uncertain.

"Just as soon as I could. I made you a promise that I intended to keep. And then once I discovered the loan was actually paid off, I tried to call several times."

She glanced away, to look out of her secret window, before returning her gaze to his. "I didn't have anything to say to you. I wouldn't let my sisters answer your call."

"Because you thought I was involved with someone else." He'd made a statement rather than asked a question.

"Yes."

"And why did the thought of another woman bother you, Pam?"

She shrugged the feminine shoulders he loved so much. "It just did."

He leaned in closer. "Do you know what I think?" Before she could respond, he said, "I think it bothered you because you realized something. Those times that we made love, I made you mine. And you know something else you might as well go ahead and accept?"

"What?" she asked tersely.

"That I love you."

She blinked. "You love me?"

"Very much. I fell in love with you the moment I set eyes on you. And I want to marry you for all the *right* reasons. I want us, the Westmorelands and the Novaks, to be a family."

She hesitated, searched his gaze for the truth in his words. He could tell from her expression the moment she found them. A smile touched her lips. "I think Jay and Raphel would have liked that."

"So will you marry me? And I might as well warn you, marrying me means getting fourteen others."

She grinned. "I don't mind because marrying me means you'll get four. Oh, and there's Iris. She's like my sister."

A deep smile touched his lips. "The more the merrier. And I might as well warn you about my fifteen Atlanta Westmoreland cousins."

"Like you said, the more the merrier," she said, shifting in his embrace to wrap her arms around his neck. "I love you, too."

He leaned in closer as his gaze zeroed in on her lips. He kissed her there, slowly at first, then a little more hungrily. And when his tongue began dueling with hers, he almost forgot where the two of them were. He pulled away from her mouth and stood with her in his arms. He then placed her on her feet.

"I think we need to let everyone know there will be a wedding after all, but not today. We will set a date when we can get all the Westmorelands in one place."

He then leaned in closer to whisper, "I'm staying at the hotel in Rosebud tonight. Do you want to come spend some time with me later?"

A satisfied smile touched her lips. "Umm, I would love to. You give. I take. No regrets."

He chuckled as he pulled her into his arms. "Yes. No regrets."

Epilogue

Pam glanced down at her wedding ring. It looked perfect on her hand. She then glanced up at her husband of ten minutes and smiled before looking around the huge, beautifully decorated ballroom at the Denver hotel. She and Dillon had decided to have a Christmas wedding and everything had turned out perfectly.

Her sisters were talking to some of Dillon's brothers and cousins and seemed to be in a very happy and festive mood. She couldn't yet distinguish which were Dillon's brothers and which ones were his cousins, since they all looked a lot alike. Even those who had traveled all the way from Atlanta. He had introduced everyone, but she was still a little fuzzy on names and faces.

And yet she had become immediate friends with

Megan, Gemma and Bailey. They simply adored their oldest cousin and let her know they were more than pleased with the woman he had chosen as his wife. And then there were the wives of the Atlanta Westmorelands, with whom she was forming lasting friendships. Last night during the rehearsal dinner she had held in her arms the newest member of the Westmoreland clan, four-month-old Jaren.

There was no doubt in anyone's mind that Dillon's cousin Jared Westmoreland and his wife, Dana, were proud of their beautiful baby girl. While holding the baby Pam had glanced up and met Dillon's gaze, and from the look he'd given her, she had a feeling that he wasn't planning on wasting any time giving her a child of her own to hold.

"Ready for our first dance, Mrs. Westmoreland?" Dillon asked, whirling her around to face him, and bringing her thoughts back to the present.

She laughed. "As ready as I'll ever be, Mr. Westmoreland."

And then he pulled her into his arms as they glided around the dance floor. Her sisters were beaming happily and that made her feel good. They had been overjoyed to hear about her wedding plans. She and Dillon had wanted a small affair but with all those Westmorelands that was impossible.

They would live in Gamble until the end of the school year, and then once Jill left for college, Pam and her sisters would move into Dillon's home in Denver. Paige and Nadia didn't have any problems with moving and

looked forward to making new friends. The house in
Gamble would be a second home for them. Pam would
be turning the day-to-day operations of the drama
academy over to the very capable hands of Cindy Ruffin.

After a few moments a deep male voice said, "May
I cut in?"

Pam glanced up into the face of the one cousin she
remembered well, because he was a nationally known
motorcycle-racing star, Thorn Westmoreland.

"Just for now," Dillon said jokingly, handing her over
to his cousin. After Thorn, she remained on the dance
floor through several more songs as each of Dillon's
male cousins got a chance to twirl her around.

Finally, she found herself back in her husband's arms
for a slow number. They would be catching a plane later
that day to Miami, where they would set sail on a cruise
to the Bahamas.

He pulled her tight into his arms and whispered, "At
last," before lowering his head and latching on to her
mouth, not caring that they had a ballroom filled with
guests. When he finally released her mouth, she couldn't
help but chuckle throatily. "That was naughty."

"No, sweetheart," he said, brushing his knuckles
gently against her cheek. "That was this Westmoreland's
way. Get used to it."

"I will." She went on tiptoe and captured his mouth
with hers, deciding to show him that Novaks had a way
of their own, as well.

* * * * *

Don't miss Ramsey's story in
HOT WESTMORELAND NIGHTS,
the next WESTMORELAND romance
from New York Times *bestselling author*
Brenda Jackson.
On sale March 2010
from Silhouette Desire®.

*Celebrate 60 years of pure reading pleasure
with Harlequin®!
Just in time for the holidays,
Silhouette Special Edition®
is proud to present*
New York Times *bestselling author*
Kathleen Eagle's
ONE COWBOY, ONE CHRISTMAS

Rodeo rider Zach Beaudry was a travelin' man—
until he broke down in middle-of-nowhere South
Dakota during a deep freeze. That's when an angel
came to his rescue....

"Don't die on me. Come on, Zel. You know how much I love you, girl. You're all I've got. Don't do this to me here. Not *now*."

But Zelda had quit on him, and Zach Beaudry had no one to blame but himself. He'd taken his sweet time hitting the road, and then miscalculated a shortcut. For all he knew he was a hundred miles from gas. But even if they were sitting next to a pump, the ten dollars he had in his pocket wouldn't get him out of South Dakota, which was not where he wanted to be right now. Not even his beloved pickup truck, Zelda, could get him much of anywhere on fumes. He was sitting out in the cold in the middle of nowhere. And getting colder.

He shifted the pickup into Neutral and pulled hard

on the steering wheel, using the downhill slope to get her off the blacktop and into the roadside grass, where she shuddered to a standstill. He stroked the padded dash. "You'll be safe here."

But Zach would not. It was getting dark, and it was already too damn cold for his cowboy ass. Zach's battered body was a barometer, and he was feeling South Dakota, big-time. He'd have given his right arm to be climbing into a hotel hot tub instead of a brutal blast of north wind. The right was his free arm anyway. Damn thing had lost altitude, touched some part of the bull and caused him a scoreless ride last time out.

It wasn't scoring him a ride this night, either. A carload of teenagers whizzed by, topping off the insult by laying on the horn as they passed him. It was at least twenty minutes before another vehicle came along. He stepped out and waved both arms this time, damn near getting himself killed. Whatever happened to *do unto others?* In places like this, decent people didn't leave each other stranded in the cold.

His face was feeling stiff, and he figured he'd better start walking before his toes went numb. He struck out for a distant yard light, the only sign of human habitation in sight. He couldn't tell how distant, but he knew he'd be hurting by the time he got there, and he was counting on some kindly old man to be answering the door. No shame among the lame.

It wasn't like Zach was fresh off the operating table—it had been a few months since his last round of repairs—but he hadn't given himself enough time. He'd lopped a couple of weeks off the near end of the doc's estimated recovery time, rigged up a brace, done some heavy-duty taping and climbed onto another bull. Hung in there for five seconds—four seconds past feeling the pop in his hip and three seconds short of the buzzer.

He could still feel the pain shooting down his leg with every step. Only this time he had to pick the damn thing up, swing it forward and drop it down again on his own.

Pride be damned, he just hoped *somebody* would be answering the door at the end of the road. The light in the front window was a good sign.

The four steps to the covered porch might as well have been four hundred, and he was looking to climb them with a lead weight chained to his left leg. His eyes were just as screwed up as his hip. Big black spots danced around with tiny red flashers, and he couldn't tell what was real and what wasn't. He stumbled over some shrubbery, steadied himself on the porch railing and peered between vertical slats.

There in the front window stood a spruce tree with a silver star affixed to the top. Zach was pretty sure the red sparks were all in his head, but the white lights twinkling by the hundreds throughout the huge tree, those were real. He wasn't too sure about the woman hanging the shiny balls. Most of her hair was caught up on her head and fastened in a curly clump, but the light captured by the escaped bits crowned her with a golden halo. Her face was a soft shadow, her body a willowy silhouette beneath a long white gown. If this was where the mind ran off to when cold started shutting down the rest of the body, then Zach's final worldly thought was, *This ain't such a bad way to go.*

If she would just turn to the window, he could die looking into the eyes of a Christmas angel.

* * * * *

Could this woman from Zach's past get the lonesome cowboy to come in from the cold...for good?
Look for
ONE COWBOY, ONE CHRISTMAS
by Kathleen Eagle.
Available December 2009
from Silhouette Special Edition®.

Copyright © 2009 by Kathleen Eagle

🎀 *Silhouette*®

SPECIAL EDITION

We're spotlighting
a different series
every month throughout 2009
to celebrate our 60th anniversary.

This December, Silhouette Special Edition® brings you

NEW YORK TIMES BESTSELLING AUTHOR
KATHLEEN EAGLE

ONE COWBOY,
ONE CHRISTMAS

Available wherever books are sold.

Visit Silhouette Books at www.eHarlequin.com

SSE60BPA

Silhouette *Desire*

New York Times Bestselling Author

SUSAN MALLERY

HIGH-POWERED, HOT-BLOODED

Innocently caught up in a corporate scandal, schoolteacher Annie McCoy has no choice but to take the tempting deal offered by ruthless CEO Duncan Patrick. Six passionate months later, Annie realizes Duncan will move on, with or without her. Now all she has to do is convince him she is the one he really wants!

Available December 2009 wherever you buy books.

ALWAYS POWERFUL, PASSIONATE AND PROVOCATIVE

Visit Silhouette Books at www.eHarlequin.com

SD76981

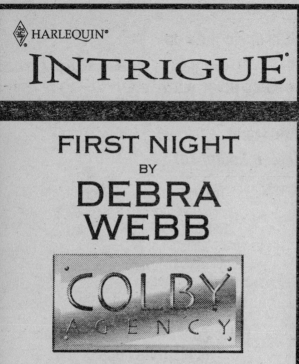

HARLEQUIN®
INTRIGUE®

FIRST NIGHT
BY
DEBRA WEBB

To prove his innocence, talented artist
Brandon Thomas is in a race against time.
Caught up in a murder investigation,
he enlists Colby agent Merrilee Walters
to help catch the true killer. If they can survive
the first night, their growing attraction
may have a chance, as well.

Available in December wherever books are sold.

www.eHarlequin.com

HI69440

Stay up-to-date on all your romance-reading news with the brand-new Harlequin *Inside Romance*!

The Harlequin
Inside Romance
is a **FREE** quarterly
newsletter highlighting
our upcoming
series releases
and promotions!

**Click on the *Inside Romance* link
on the front page of
www.eHarlequin.com
or e-mail us at
InsideRomance@Harlequin.ca
to sign up to receive
your FREE newsletter today!**

You can also subscribe by writing to us at: HARLEQUIN BOOKS
Attention: Customer Service Department
P.O. Box 9057, Buffalo, NY 14269-9057

Please allow 4-6 weeks for delivery of the first issue by mail.

IRNBPAQ309

HARLEQUIN®

A Cowboy Christmas
Marin Thomas

2 stories in 1!

The holidays are a rough time for widower
Logan Taylor and single dad Fletcher McFadden—
neither hunky cowboy has been lucky in love.
But Christmas is the season of miracles! Logan
meets his match in "A Christmas Baby," while
Fletcher gets a second chance at love in "Marry
Me, Cowboy." This year both cowboys are on
Santa's Nice list!

Available December
wherever books are sold.

"LOVE, HOME & HAPPINESS"

www.eHarlequin.com

HAR75292

HQN™

We *are* romance™

New York Times and USA TODAY bestselling author

SUSAN MALLERY

**brings you the final tale
in the Lone Star Sisters series.**

All that stands between
Garth Duncan and his
goal of taking down his
cruel businessman father,
Jed Titan, is Deputy
Dana Birch, her gun
and a growing passion
that can't be denied....

Hot on Her Heels

Available now!

www.HQNBooks.com

PHSM384

REQUEST YOUR FREE BOOKS!

2 FREE NOVELS PLUS 2 FREE GIFTS!

Silhouette® Desire®

Passionate, Powerful, Provocative!

YES! Please send me 2 FREE Silhouette Desire® novels and my 2 FREE gifts (gifts are worth about $10). After receiving them, if I don't wish to receive any more books, I can return the shipping statement marked "cancel". If I don't cancel, I will receive 6 brand-new novels every month and be billed just $4.05 per book in the U.S. or $4.74 per book in Canada. That's a savings of almost 15% off the cover price! It's quite a bargain! Shipping and handling is just 50¢ per book.* I understand that accepting the 2 free books and gifts places me under no obligation to buy anything. I can always return a shipment and cancel at any time. Even if I never buy another book, the two free books and gifts are mine to keep forever.   225 SDN EYMS   326 SDN EYM4

Name	(PLEASE PRINT)	
Address		Apt. #
City	State/Prov.	Zip/Postal Code

Signature (if under 18, a parent or guardian must sign)

Mail to the Silhouette Reader Service:
IN U.S.A.: P.O. Box 1867, Buffalo, NY 14240-1867
IN CANADA: P.O. Box 609, Fort Erie, Ontario L2A 5X3

Not valid to current subscribers of Silhouette Desire books.

Want to try two free books from another line?
Call 1-800-873-8635 or visit www.morefreebooks.com.

* Terms and prices subject to change without notice. Prices do not include applicable taxes. Sales tax applicable in N.Y. Canadian residents will be charged applicable provincial taxes and GST. Offer not valid in Quebec. This offer is limited to one order per household. All orders subject to approval. Credit or debit balances in a customer's account(s) may be offset by any other outstanding balance owed by or to the customer. Please allow 4 to 6 weeks for delivery. Offer available while quantities last.

Your Privacy: Silhouette Books is committed to protecting your privacy. Our Privacy Policy is available online at www.eHarlequin.com or upon request from the Reader Service. From time to time we make our lists of customers available to reputable third parties who may have a product or service of interest to you. If you would prefer we not share your name and address, please check here. ☐

SDES09R

Silhouette Desire

COMING NEXT MONTH
Available December 8, 2009

#1981 HIGH-POWERED, HOT-BLOODED—Susan Mallery
Man of the Month
Crowned the country's meanest CEO, he needs a public overhaul.
His solution: a sweet-natured kindergarten teacher who will turn
him into an angel...though he's having a devil of a time keeping
his hands off her!

#1982 THE MAVERICK—Diana Palmer
Long, Tall Texans
Cowboy Harley Fowler is in the midst of mayhem—is seduction
the answer? Don't miss this story of a beloved hero readers have
been waiting to see fall in love!

#1983 LONE STAR SEDUCTION—Day Leclaire
Texas Cattleman's Club: Maverick County Millionaires
He finally has everything he's always wanted within his grasp.
He just can't allow himself to fall for the one woman who nearly
destroyed his empire...no matter how much he still wants her.

#1984 TO TAME HER TYCOON LOVER—Ann Major
Foolishly she'd given her innocence to the rich boy next door...
only to have her heart broken. Years later, she's vowed not to fall
for his seductive ways again. But she'd forgotten the tycoon's
undeniable magnetism and pure determination.

#1985 MILLIONAIRE UNDER THE MISTLETOE—
Tessa Radley
After unexpectedly sleeping with her family's secret benefactor,
she's taken by surprise when he proposes a more permanent
arrangement—as his wife!

#1986 DEFIANT MISTRESS, RUTHLESS MILLIONAIRE—
Yvonne Lindsay
Bent on ruining his father's company, he lures his new assistant
away from the man. But the one thing he never expects is a
double-cross! Will she stick to her mission or fall victim to her
new boss's seduction?

SDCNMBPA1109